100 MUST-READ

# SCIENCE FICTIONNOVELS

Stephen E. Andrews and Nick Rennison

Foreword by Christopher Priest

A & C Black · London

First published 2006
A & C Black Publishers Limited
38 Soho Square
London W1D 3HB
www.acblack.com

ISBN-10: 0–7136–7585–3
ISBN-13: 978–0–7136–7585–6

A CIP catalogue record for this book is available from
the British Library.

This book is produced using paper that is made from wood grown in
managed, sustainable forests. It is natural, renewable and recyclable.
The logging and manufacturing processes conform to the environmental
regulations of the country of origin.

Typeset in 8.5pt on 12pt Meta-Light

Printed and bound in Great Britain by
Bookmarque Ltd, Croydon, Surrey

# CONTENTS

# FOREWORD

If you're looking for a reliable guide to what science fiction is, you have come to the right place. This is a book that contains a list of the one hundred irreplaceable books from the science fiction genre.

But it is also rather more than just a list, because not only is each book lucidly introduced, summarized and placed in its general context, there are many 'read on' suggestions. These will take the interested reader down a number of sidetracks to distant literary places, some of which will come as a surprise to many people. The net that contains SF is a big one and fantastic literature can be cast over a wide area. Not everything is obvious.

Beyond even the recommendations, there is an argument that runs throughout the book. It gently explains, defines, promotes, defends science fiction, always with a civilized enthusiasm and from a position of authority.

When I discovered the genre long ago, late in my teens, there were far fewer SF books to read than there are now. In fact it felt (perhaps falsely) that with a little dedication it would be possible to sit down and read everything that had ever been published. I never attempted the feat, although when I encountered some of the more serious science fiction fans I did wonder if they were trying it.

In the early to middle 1960s, most of the science fiction that then existed had been written for magazines. SF was predominantly a short-story form, and novels were comparatively rare. The few there were had almost all first appeared as serials, which is how many of the older novels on the main list in this book were published.

To return to the story of my own brief contact with reading science fiction, I devoured the books avidly for a few years, but by the time I was in my mid-twenties my tastes had become more complex and not long after that I stopped reading science fiction almost completely. (Almost completely, because for several years I was a publisher's professional reader, and throughout my career I have occasionally reviewed new books.) It always feels to me as if I gave up before I had seriously tackled the subject.

I was surprised to discover, therefore, when I read this long list compiled by Messrs Andrews and Rennison, that I had read almost half of the books here.

Naturally, they tend to be the older ones, but not entirely.

Do I agree with the choices on the main list? Yes and no. I would like to have seen J.G. Ballard's stories given prominence over his novels. He is still an under-rated writer, and that is because people judge him by his novels: on his scale, the B-list. There ought to be a Richard Cowper book here: *The Twilight of Briareus* or *The Road to Corlay*, or his stories. The same from Robert Sheckley, who was one of the finest 20th century short story writers, but whose novels weren't as good. I would have chosen John Wyndham's *The Day of the Triffids* or *The Kraken*

*Wakes* over *The Midwich Cuckoos*. Aldiss's *Greybeard* rather than *Hothouse*. Dick's *The Man in the High Castle*.

What would I have left out? The Asimovs and the Heinleins, certainly, since in completely different ways they did much to distract everyone from the idea that science fiction should be written well. (This is a personal view – the consensus of the SF world is against me.) The novels by 'Doc' Smith, Jack Williamson and Raymond F. Jones are period pieces, and belong in a museum. Including two novels by Alfred Bester is including one too many, but *The Stars my Destination* is probably central to the entire SF argument. And H.G. Wells's *The Island of Doctor Moreau* is famous, while not being one of his best books.

On the whole, though, I go along with the selections here.

I have long argued that science fiction is not something that should be judged as a unitary form. Any generalized argument in favour of SF, no matter how well or strenuously mounted, can be instantly undermined by pointing at one of the genre's many, many embarrassments. (The opposite is also true, but not as subversively enjoyable to do.)

Much better to think of SF as a place where adventurous or original writers can take advantage of certain blessings practically unique in literature: an articulate, faithful and intelligent readership, an active professional market for short stories, a consistent commercial niche within publishing and bookselling, a body of literary criticism that is both knowledgeable about the literature and expectant of high quality. This is the sort of literary environment where writers can practise, where they can develop their individual voices and be heard, encouraged and soon relished.

That is the best way to read and understand this book: as an introduction not to a genre that might or might not be to everyone's taste, but as a recommendation of the works of authors who are not known to many people outside the genre.

There are many surprises here, in that sense. Nearly one hundred of them, in fact.

**Christopher Priest**

# ABOUTTHISBOOK

This book is not intended to provide a list of the 100 'best' SF novels. A definitive list of the greatest SF novels is an impossibility – personal tastes in SF, as in any area of writing, differ and any 'Best of...' list is always unacceptably subjective. We have been guided instead by the title of our book and have chosen 100 books to read in order to gain an overview of the rich and diverse writing to be found in SF.

The Introduction, on the evolution and proliferation of SF, provides a useful background to understanding references in the entries to movements and moments in SF's history – there is also a short glossary of definitions on page 176. The entries, arranged A to Z by author, describe the plot of each title while aiming to avoid too many 'spoilers', offer some value judgements and describe the author's place in the history of SF and/or their other works. The symbol >> before an author name (e.g. >> **J.G. Ballard**) indicates that one or more of their books is covered in the A to Z author entries, suggesting to the reader the option of turning immediately to the relevant entries to explore that particular writer's work and place in SF history.

Each entry is followed by a 'Read on' list, which includes books by the same author, books by stylistically similar writers or books on a theme relevant to the entry. We have also noted significant film versions (with dates of release), where applicable. 'Read on a Theme' listings are designed to help you explore a particular area of SF in greater depth, and at the end of the book you will find listings relating to film, music and key awards. Space dictated that most entries be kept short, and for more detailed information on the writers you may like to consult *The Encyclopedia of Science Fiction* (ed. John Clute and Peter Nicholls).

We aimed to produce a book that would be useful as a starting point for exploring the genre and, in order to do this, we decided that we needed to cover all the major themes of SF – from perennial ideas you might expect from experience of the mass media to more unusual concepts that rarely appear in the genre outside books. This is why some authors are not represented by what are usually considered their best books. It is also why most authors have only one book. This approach caused us some difficulties, especially in the cases of writers who are both prolific and brilliant. Robert Silverberg, for example, is one of a number of writers represented here who, it could be argued, deserves a second selection. Even authors of particular significance like Philip K. Dick had to be limited to two entries. Only H.G. Wells, we decided, whose status as the founding father of modern SF makes him unique, should have three entries. In our final choice of books, we focused on titles that we thought both representative of particular themes in SF and singularly important to the development of the genre.

We believe SF to be a genre that thrives on debate and we have excluded a number of canonical works and writers at the expense of books and authors whom we feel deserve greater exposure in the hope that this will stimulate it. We have also ignored the constraints of our title by including two short story collections, which we believe are essential to a full understanding of the history of SF. In this, we were also influenced by the fact that the two writers (John W. Campbell and Harlan Ellison) have been regularly excluded from earlier lists, largely because their finest work is in short story form.

We have tried to select books that are reprinted regularly. A trip to your local bookshop armed with a list of your chosen titles should be enough for a bookseller to check their availability for you. We were delighted to find that a large number of classic SF titles were in print either in the USA or UK at the time this book went to press. However, the commercial reality of publishing is such that many classics do remain out of print for years on end, only reaching readers via the goodwill of committed editors at major publishers and dedicated fanatics at small presses. None the less, due to print-on-demand technology and the generally easy availability of out-of-print titles and imports via the internet, hours of scouring second-hand bookshops for that elusive masterpiece should only be an enjoyably serendipitous last resort.

## ACKNOWLEDGEMENTS

The authors would like to thank Patricia Jones, Eve Gorton, David & Margaret Andrews, Christopher Priest, Yvonne Aburrow, Heather Bird, Graham Bray, Martin Folkes, Simon Hemmings, Colin Litster, Judy Tither, Peter Waterman, Ian Watson and everyone at A & C Black, especially Jenny Ridout, Katie Taylor, Caroline Ball and Suzi Nicolaou.

# INTRODUCTION

Science fiction has always been an infamously difficult genre to define. Today, after decades of blockbuster movies and popular television series, defining SF (as I will refer to science fiction from now on) is harder than ever. Almost everyone has his or her definition of what SF is – and almost everyone's definition is inadequate. SF writing, in particular, is broader in scope and maturer in execution (as well as older) than anyone judging the genre solely on its manifestations in film and television would realize.

Popular misconceptions of SF are understandable, since much of it was published contemporaneously with the growth in the technology that has allowed both the mass media to flourish and SF itself to conquer extra-literary media. Written SF has, therefore, long been in competition with the more accessible 'sci-fi' of other media. Since the mid-seventies – a period when written SF reached a point of complexity and seriousness that belied some of its humble origins – the genre has been excessively dominated by cinema, TV and computer games. Less visible to the majority of people in print than it has been in the mass media, SF has come to be defined, in the popular imagination, by its appearances in cinema and television. Books have been a neglected poor relation of competing media with more surface glamour. Ironically, written SF has become a victim of its own prophecies of all-conquering technologies. The seductive hi-tech of Playstation® and the CGI special effects of Hollywood blockbusters have made paperbacks look old-fashioned to generations raised on the immediacy of screens. Books involve more effort from their audience but they offer levels of reward and quality scarce in other media.

So, the current popular opinion of SF writing is that it is a literature of implausible adolescent entertainment, fixated on gleaming starships and absurd zap guns, gimmicky time machines, clunky robots and slimy aliens. This perception is a narrow and inaccurate one, based largely on ignorance. Written SF matured a long time ago; mass media SF often still seems to be wrestling with a protracted puberty. This is not to say there is no great SF outside books – directors like Stanley Kubrick and Ridley Scott, auteurs like David Cronenberg, scriptwriters like Nigel Kneale and rock musicians like David Bowie and Hawkwind are just a few examples of first-rate artists who have worked primarily in mass media SF. The focus of this book is on written SF but we have ensured that the books we have included in this guide are some of the most exciting and stimulating reads in the history of fiction, many of which will appeal to readers whose experience of SF is not predominantly literary. The term 'novel' has the same roots as the word 'novelty', something of which there is no shortage in SF. What follows in this guide will be far from dry, worthy and dull. We can be confident in claiming that you're in for a wild ride.

Before attempting our own definition of SF, we need to examine its history. As the above makes clear, there has been a myriad of arguments over the decades about what SF is, and there is no consensus. This is healthy. Like all good fiction, SF is enriched by debate. My personal opinion is that it is the definitive literature of change itself. We have seen more of that in the past 200 years than in the whole of previous human history and it is into that past that we need to travel in search of the origins of the genre.

## BACK TO THE FUTURE

Some commentators have argued that SF first appears in antiquity, with works such as *The Epic of Gilgamesh* (circa 2000BC), which features flying machines and *The True History of Lucian* by the Greek author Lucian (circa AD140–180) which covers a trip to the moon and a war in space. However, these and other works of what has been called 'proto-SF' probably owe as much to mythology and magic as they do to technology. This places Lucian and other pioneers of astounding voyages to strange places firmly in the realm of fantasy writing rather than SF. The Greek legend of Prometheus, who stole fire from the gods and was eternally punished for the gift of knowledge he gave to mankind, could also be a template for some future SF writing. However, most people would argue that mythology and the supernatural are, by definition, unscientific. Since most proto-SF depends on one or the other, it may have to be excluded from the genre.

While the modern novel gradually emerged from medieval chivalric romances (which played a central role in the development of the fantasy genre), many writers continued to tell tales of voyages to other worlds and some described perfect societies in philosophical works such as Thomas More's *Utopia* (1516). Some, such as Jonathan Swift's *Gulliver's Travels* (1726), satirized their own culture by using the metaphor of imperfect societies. (One of the best ways to try to understand the complex and sometimes absurd nature of our world is via a distorting mirror of reality that uses exaggeration to draw our attention to the pivotal events and assumptions of the society that shapes our lives. SF may often be set in the future or on other worlds, but it is often using these settings as symbolic of our present.)

However, many critics have argued that SF itself could not exist before the age of scientific method, when accurate observation, rigorous theorizing and repeated proof-making experimentation became the key to technological advance. Before the Enlightenment in the 18th century, tradition and organized religion had checked the forward momentum of knowledge, but the combined social impact of the French Revolution and the innovations of the Industrial Age created the ideal conditions for fiction truly conscious of science to flourish. (It is worth noting here that both social and technological change are central to SF, so to think of the genre only in relation to the 'hard' sciences of physics, engineering, biology and chemistry is a mistake. Other disciplines inevitably have an effect on human beings and SF can also encompass the 'soft' sciences of sociology, psychology, politics and philosophy.)

The final condition that set the stage for the arrival of 'true' SF was the major trend in early 19th-century arts: Romanticism. Romanticism was a reaction against the rationalism of the Enlightenment but it succeeded in incorporating some of the ideals of 18th-century thinking into its own new outlook. Romanticism continued to encourage people to enjoy the new intellectual freedom the disciplines of science fostered but it insisted there should also be a focus on the sublime and the wondrous. Although the impact of Romanticism was most strongly felt in poetry and music, it had its effect on fiction, particularly on the form known as the Gothic novel. The power of Gothic writers lay in their willingness to dream and to encourage the kind of 'sense of wonder' that has coloured SF ever since the appearance of a book many commentators (notably ›› Brian Aldiss) have identified as the first true SF novel: ›› Mary Shelley's 1818 *Frankenstein* (The entry on Shelley examines this argument.)

As the Industrial Revolution gathered pace, SF novels became more common. Speculations on future wars were particularly popular as the implications of more efficient machines and weapons became clear. Utopias also flourished as new political ideas such as socialism began to develop, notably *News From Nowhere* (1890) by the artist, poet and craftsman William Morris and *Erewhon* by Samuel Butler (1872). Other new sciences encouraged writers to work on fresh themes. Robert Louis Stevenson's *The Strange Case of Dr Jekyll and Mr Hyde* (1886), for example, uses pharmacology as a basis for physical and mental transformation that allowed the author to meditate upon the balance of good and evil in man and the potentially destructive power of new knowledge.

Most significant in the formulation of what most people today would recognize as SF were the careers of the American author Edgar Allan Poe (1809–49) and the Frenchman ›› Jules Verne (1828–1905). Poe was probably the most important writer in the history of genre fiction and was a pioneer of detective fiction, horror and fantasy as well as SF. He wrote short stories almost exclusively (his only novel, *The Narrative of Arthur Gordon Pym* is a 'hollow Earth' SF story) in a dense Gothic-Romantic style that inspired writers interested in the bizarre. The emotional intensity of his prose and the melodramatic influence of his alcohol-induced depressions brought a decadent outsider element to the genre. Verne, meanwhile, produced numerous direct, optimistic and adventurous novels from the 1860s onward that had a massive influence over magazine writers to come. Verne dubbed his works 'voyages extraordinaires' and they include such classics as *Journey to the Centre of the Earth*, *From the Earth to the Moon* and *Twenty Thousand Leagues Under the Sea*. The fact that many of Verne's novels (*Around the World in Eighty Days*, for instance) are straight-forward exploration stories with no SF elements and that many of his books were massive bestsellers explains how SF and adventure became synonymous in the popular imagination.

At the end of the 19th century, while Verne was the undisputed master of the as yet unnamed genre, the Englishman ➤➤ H.G. Wells started producing the ground-breaking books that cemented his reputation as the father of modern SF. Wells described *The Time Machine*, *The War of the Worlds* and *The Invisible Man* (among many others that helped expand what have become perennial themes of SF) as 'scientific romances' in order to distinguish them from the social and character-based novels that dominated the fiction of his day. Wells knew his fiction was not realism but, by using the term 'scientific', he was affirming that his work had its basis in the rational yet currently improbable, rather than in the magical and the impossible. He was speculating and extrapolating from the knowledge of his day to suggest the possibilities of tomorrow. His excellent prose skills, the plausibility of his imagination, his fierce intelligence and his literary versatility (Wells was also a distinguished social novelist who explored the new middle classes, feminism and left-wing politics) have ensured that he remains the undisputed Grand Master SF writer for all time.

## AMAZING STORIES

Some commentators (particularly ›› Norman Spinrad) have argued that the history of SF is the history of how it has been marketed, suggesting that if writing is published with the label 'science fiction' on its binding, then it is SF, and a book not marketed as such is not SF. This may seem an obvious point but it is a useful one to make. By the early twentieth century, the cheap magazines known as 'pulps' (named after the inexpensive paper they were printed on) flooded the news stands of America. The pulps covered genres such as crime, adventure and westerns. Between the Edwardian era and the end of the First World War, writers like ›› Edgar Rice Burroughs (*Tarzan of the Apes*), Robert E. Howard (*Conan the Barbarian*) and H.P. Lovecraft (The *Cthulhu Mythos* stories) were setting the standards for pulp writing in the fantasy genre and occasionally producing the odd SF tale. Meanwhile ›› E.E. 'Doc' Smith was starting to write 'space operas'. All the elements of *Star Wars*, the cultural artefact most people today would cite as an example of SF, were present in Smith's classic works, which is an indication of how far the cinematic and television versions of the genre have trailed behind written SF.

Publisher Hugo Gernsback took a decisive step by naming the genre in his editorial for the first issue of his magazine *Amazing Stories* (1926). He called it 'scientifiction', using the works of Wells, Verne and Poe as examples of what he meant by this new word. By 1929, this unwieldy term had mutated into 'science fiction'. (Experts have identified European magazines up to fifty years older as exclusively SF magazines and have discovered that a poetry critic used the term even earlier but Gernsback deserves the credit as the first editor to label his publications as 'science fiction'.)

Gernsback was more interested in technological accuracy than literary quality. Verne's adventure writing, the themes of extraterrestrial life and time travel explored so eloquently by Wells and the lurid, verbose style of Poe came together in Gernsback's optimistic vision. Science fiction as a publishing category had finally appeared and, through the beliefs of Gernsback and his successor, ›› John W. Campbell Jr, magazine-based SF separated itself from mainstream fiction to become a distinct literary genre. Daring themes such as robotics, faster-than-light travel, ESP, computers, parallel worlds and so on became commonplace in genre SF. With notable exceptions, SF in the mainstream has been more conservative in its speculations.

Many believe this separation did more harm than good, turning the genre tradition into a ghetto, its stories regarded by general readers as a commercially driven, immature form of fiction (›› Thomas M. Disch has even proposed the idea that SF is a kind of children's literature). There is some truth in this viewpoint. The poorer examples of pulp SF undoubtedly contributed to the popular idea, still dominant in the media, of SF as childish escapism. But genre SF still possesses a raw energy in its execution and an intellectual audacity in its themes that can make most general fiction seem stilted and mundane by comparison. Some genre SF is very well written indeed. Literary snobbery and pseudo-intellectual ignorance have played their part in damning the magazine tradition as entirely unworthy of serious consideration.

Other commentators have expressed a wish to see genre SF rejoin the mainstream from which it diverged, claiming that it is a specifically American model. The true home of SF, in this argument, is Britain. The importance of Swift, Shelley and other writers such as Richard Jefferies (his *After London, Wild England* (1885) inspired the particularly English disaster novel popularized among general readers by ›› John Wyndham) in the formation of the genre adds weight to this argument. Writers working outside the pulps (such as ›› Aldous Huxley, Olaf Stapledon and ›› George Orwell) continued to produce Wellsian titles enjoyed by general readers and this tendency continues today. There is a huge list of SF novels that have been produced by writers working outside any genre tradition.

In 1937, John W. Campbell was appointed editor of *Astounding*, bringing a new discipline to Gernsback's vision. Campbell rivalled E.E. Smith as a writer of space opera but, despite his insistence on accurate science, he also had an eye for good prose and storytelling talent, encouraging and discovering the writers who are usually credited with defining modern genre SF. Our entry on Campbell details his significance as the architect of what fans now call the Golden Age.

Campbell's domination of SF continued until the end of the 1940s and the launch of two ground-breaking magazines that brought new levels of intellectual sophistication, literary style and more adult subject matter to the genre. *Galaxy* and *The Magazine of Fantasy & Science*

*Fiction* fostered new authors eager to break with Campbell and his acolytes, some of whom had already produced their definitive works. The Holocaust, atomic bombs and the subsequent Cold War, and the mysterious appearance of flying saucers, ushered in new fears about the way our world was going and provided rich areas for writers to explore. The post-war economic boom in America that produced the consumer culture, the birth of rock and roll, and the widespread availability of TV also broadened the scope for SF that was more focused on the human sciences. Horace Gold at *Galaxy* and Anthony Boucher at *Fantasy & Science Fiction* were sophisticated editors, ready to encourage writers keen to tackle this brave new world.

Genre SF novels now appeared as books for the first time, having previously been limited to publication as magazine serials. Although paperbacks threatened the pulps so much that they would be all but extinct by the end of the fifties, genre SF flourished as never before or since. ›› Alfred Bester introduced dazzling wordplay, ›› Frederik Pohl and C.M Kornbluth added sociology, ›› Philip José Farmer broke sexual taboos and ›› Ray Bradbury's poetic approach won over mainstream critics, while ›› Philip K. Dick threw dice with reality in his wild explorations of human perception. In Britain, traditional SF masters like ›› Arthur C. Clarke saw their popularity and expertise grow and John Wyndham became the first example of a genre writer crossing back into the mainstream bestseller list by using a more accessible style that general readers loved. Both Clarke and Wyndham had been active as writers before the Second World War and they paved the way for newcomers in the late fifties like Brian Aldiss and ›› J.G. Ballard. British genre SF was curated by E.J. Carnell, editor of *New Worlds*, the UK equivalent of *Astounding* and *Galaxy* rolled into one.

# BRAVE NEW WORLDS, BOLD NEW WAVE OR FROM NEW WAVE TO CYBERPUNK

By the early sixties the paperback was king and only the best magazines survived. The next generation of SF writers, emerging at the end of the previous decade, was even more willing to challenge the status quo. Instrumental in sparking the revolution in SF that became known as New Wave (a term appropriated by ›› Christopher Priest from French experimental cinema) was ›› Michael Moorcock, a young fantasy writer who believed that experimental author ›› William S. Burroughs was pointing the way forward to a bolder, more mature SF and that only Ballard and Aldiss were following the lead he was providing. Much of the best SF has always been, metaphorically at least, about the present rather than the future and Burroughs was the one mainstream author of stature (admirers compared him to James Joyce) who was using the satirical and polemical potential of SF to greatest effect.

Moorcock took over the editorship of *New Worlds* in 1964, steering the magazine away from pulp into daring, innovative explorations of drugs, sex, time, politics and art. Moorcock's anti-heroic stance encouraged powerful young American writers such as Thomas M. Disch, ›› John Sladek and Norman Spinrad to move to Swinging London to join him, alongside home-grown talent like Aldiss, Ballard and ›› M. John Harrison, in making genre SF part of the counterculture, inspired by experimental modernist literature, Pop Art, the civil rights movement, the Cuban missile crisis, the Kennedy assassination, Vietnam, the Pill, feminism, psychedelic drugs and rock music. In America, the hippies made not only Tolkien's fantasy *The Lord of the Rings* but also SF works like ›› Robert A. Heinlein's *Stranger in a*

*Strange Land* and ❯❯ Frank Herbert's *Dune* into massive bestsellers.

Maverick short-story writer ❯❯ Harlan Ellison announced he was editing a ground-breaking anthology entitled *Dangerous Visions*. Joined by contemporaries like ❯❯ Robert Silverberg, ❯❯ Samuel R. Delany (the first major black SF author), ❯❯ Roger Zelazny, ❯❯ Ursula K. Le Guin (the finest female writer of SF to date) and some of the *New Worlds* writers, plus established masters like Philip K. Dick and Philip José Farmer, the mercurial Ellison pushed the envelope with this book and it became the focus of the American New Wave.

It now seemed that anything was possible in SF and that the genre would triumphantly rejoin the mainstream. Female writers became more visible, some (like hardcore feminist ❯❯ Joanna Russ) entering SF via the New Wave. Before this time, most publishers of SF magazines regarded their market as composed primarily of young males and consequently courted writers and writing that appealed to a masculine sensibility. Few women had been accepted as pulp writers, so male authors had a head start in exploring the thematic possibilities of the genre. By the sixties, many of the recurrent ideas of genre SF had been thoroughly explored except from feminist angles. As SF is a modernist genre and modernism acclaims the pioneers of new ideas, this was another advantage male writers enjoyed until the New Wave. Additionally, many women choosing a career in imaginative fiction elected to write fantasy instead. Some women authors, like Anne McCaffrey, even write SF that, because of its use of magical symbolism such as dragons, reads like fantasy. Although the high quality of writing by many female SF writers is indisputable, these historical circumstances provide the main explanation for the relatively small number of women authors represented in this book.

For the same reasons, important writers of alternative sexualities and of non-Caucasian ethnicity were also scarce in SF publishing before the New Wave. Since the dawn of the seventies, far more women and those of sexual and racial minorities have written and read SF, but the influence of the mass youth culture in popularizing the genre ensured that big publishing houses and film studios would continue to put their commercial focus on traditional SF written by white Anglo-Saxon males, many of them by now famous. Genre SF entered the realms of big business as elder statesmen like Asimov, Clarke, Heinlein and Herbert commanded huge advances from publishers and produced massive bestsellers. New Wave writers like Ballard, Priest and >> Keith Roberts worked hard at blurring the boundaries between genre SF and main-stream literature in Britain and the *Dangerous Visions* contributors watched their awards pile high as their audacity became an acceptable facet of American SF. Hard SF made a comeback as the decade pro-gressed. Writers with engineering backgrounds like >> Larry Niven followed the traditional right-wing model established by Robert Heinlein, while other scientist-authors like >> Joe Haldeman and >> Gregory Benford produced SF that showed the influence of both conservative and New Wave writing.

By the late seventies, written SF seemed to be running out of steam and the fantasy publishing boom began to gather pace. Once, it would have been impossible for even a large bookshop to shelve fantasy separately, as 'sword and sorcery' (the most popular variant of the genre) was written only by a handful of authors. Fantasies ended up being shelved with SF and, indeed, some seminal authors wrote variants of both. However, since the early eighties, fantasies have become as common as SF paperbacks and the dividing lines between them have become increasingly blurred, contributing greatly to public misconception of SF as predominantly clichéd, juvenile material. For, although there are many excellent fantasy works that should be sampled by all kinds of readers, the large majority of such books are highly derivative and formulaic, merely riffing on *The Lord of the Rings*. In the age of the pulp magazines, fantasy and SF were published in different periodicals (with only a handful of exceptions), again an indication that editors had established there were two distinct genre markets to serve. Today, bookshops, recent marketing by publishers and journalists who habitually use contradictory labels such as 'science fiction fantasy' have all contributed to this muddying of the genre waters and SF fans themselves have not always helped when they have impishly voted for the occasional fantasy novel as a Hugo award winner, further confusing the general reader.

In the late seventies *Star Wars*, *Close Encounters of the Third Kind* and *ET* thrillingly revitalized popular cinema, but they contributed to the simultaneous commercial success and dumbing-down of genre SF, as mediocre tie-in books became bestsellers. On the other hand, bold, superb films like *Alien*, *Blade Runner* and *Videodrome* partially inspired the next generation of American genre writers, who sought to find a true hybrid between hard science and New Wave experimentalism. These were the cyberpunks. Their understanding of the coming information age combined with an attitude derived from the rock groups of the era brought a blast of cold, thin air into the lungs of readers. ❯❯ William Gibson, ❯❯ Bruce Sterling and ❯❯ Pat Cadigan brought an exhilarating postmodern edge to genre SF that made the mainstream critics (used by now to the literary ability of the British New Wave) sit up and take notice. Cyberpunk engaged with virtual reality, body modification, artificial intelligence and urban blight in a manner that was stunningly contemporary. Sterling's *Mirrorshades* anthology was the manifesto for this new angle of attack. Almost twenty years later *The Matrix* appeared, instantly popularizing cyberpunk concepts that had been around in written SF for a long time.

Young British writers responded to cyberpunk by using the post-*New Worlds* magazine *Interzone* to launch a new British renaissance in radical hard SF in the late eighties, emboldened by the success of ›› Iain M. Banks. (An unfortunate effect of this was that New Wave veterans were occasionally left out in the cold – Keith Roberts, Christopher Priest and M. John Harrison were often marketed and published as writers of general fiction, which lost them sales to less well-informed genre readers.) Fantasy fiction continued to flourish, restricting the shelf space and publisher spending previously earmarked for SF. Readers in the nineties did, however, embrace the likes of ›› Peter F. Hamilton, Dan Simmons and ›› Michael Swanwick, whose galaxy-spanning adventures and ease with the language of technology updated the space opera for the internet generation. While many find the new radical hard SF and postmillennial cyberpunk of today exhilarating, others claim that its occasional technobabble has returned SF to the genre ghetto it occupied before the New Wave. Another argument would be that SF has actually won its battle for credibility without sacrificing its outsider status: mobile phones, PCs, iPods, cosmetic surgery and newscasts about cloning and environmental crisis are all around us. We live in a world that SF predicted. SF themes also continue to reinvigorate the mainstream, with books like *Cloud Atlas*, *The Time Traveller's Wife*, *Oryx and Crake* and *Never Let Me Go*, all of which borrow from SF, filling the bestseller charts in the Sunday supplements.

## SF, MORE THAN SCI-FI

After this swift précis of the history of SF, it should be easier to agree a definition. But even the label itself remains uncertain. Judith Merril, Heinlein, Ellison and Margaret Atwood have argued that the term 'speculative fiction' should be used instead of 'science fiction' in order to broaden the possibilities for the genre so that works outside the technology-fixated Campbellian tradition can be included. Critic Robert Scholes has suggested 'structural fabulation', a highly technical literary term that allows closer connections with mainstream postmodernism and fantasy. The mass media prefers the flippant and dismissively pejorative 'sci-fi' but hardcore readers dislike its association with the poorer TV series and clichéd movies. I suggest that ambiguously calling the genre 'SF', without an insistence on a firm decoding of the term, will allow the audience to find their own personal meaning.

Author Damon Knight said that science fiction is what we point at when we say the words. I feel that any all-encompassing definition would involve a sense of the historical progression of the genre from *Frankenstein* onwards but would point to ideas of 'conceptual break-through' and 'paradigm shift' as the essential meat of SF. The genre inevitably involves the reader (and often the characters in the story) breaking through into a new understanding of the universe or in a fresh situation unlike any humankind has previously encountered. SF stories often begin with an unfamiliar worldview (or paradigm) that shifts our consciousness into looking at the universe in a fresh way. For example, what if there were a scientist who could create a man by combining electrical engineering, chemistry, dubious surgical techniques and parts of dead bodies? The impact of such an innovation would change our society into something fundamentally different. The possibilities of today's genetic engineering technology imply that soon *Frankenstein* may be more than just science fiction....

The debate about what SF is will continue but I'm confident that, by the time you've read this book and our suggested novels, you'll have discovered dozens of superb, entertaining writers and you'll be able to start deciding for yourself what science fiction is. By that time, the real world will resemble an SF novel even more closely than it does already. For now, I'll conclude this introduction with my own definition of SF:

*SF is the literature that suggests the significant, scientifically explicable changes that may potentially occur in the sphere of human knowledge and experience, exploring how they might affect our minds, bodies and culture.*

Happy reading.

Stephen E. Andrews
Bath, 2006

# A-ZOFENTRIES

## BRIAN ALDISS (b. 1925) UK

### HOTHOUSE (1962)

At some point in the far future the Earth has become fixed in its orbit in such a way that one side faces continually towards the sun and the other remains shrouded in perpetual darkness. The result has been a radical alteration in the flora and fauna on the planet. The sunward side of the Earth is largely given over to plants and it is dominated by the vast efflorescence of a gigantic, multi-levelled tree. While the vegetation and plant species, many of them weird and wonderful, and brilliantly described by Aldiss, have flourished, human life has retreated to one of the lowest rungs of the ecological ladder. Stranded amid the fecund jungle of the future, and surrounded by the berrywhisks, trapper-snappers, oystermaws and wiltmilts of Aldiss's imagination, the green-skinned descendants of man have to struggle to survive. The story focuses on a boy named Gren who is taken away from his tribe and comes into contact with an intelligent fungus intent on using humans for its own purposes. Linked to the fungus in a symbiotic relationship, Gren and others are led on a journey that eventually takes them to the dark side of the planet.

Like **Non-Stop**, Aldiss's first SF novel, *Hothouse* follows a human quest to understand the nature of the world. The narrative is driven forward by Gren's voyage further and further into the unknown but what the reader eventually remembers of *Hothouse* is not so much the quest itself as the inventiveness with which Aldiss creates his alternative world. Aldiss has been an important figure in British SF for close on half a century and his *Helliconia* trilogy, first published in the 1980s, is an epic vision of the rise and fall of civilizations but his earlier novels, of which *Hothouse* is a fine example, can scarcely be matched for the sense of wonder and astonishment they evoke.

### ≋ Read on
*Non-Stop, Frankenstein Unbound, The Saliva Tree*
Michael Coney, *The Ultimate Jungle*; Robert Holdstock, *Mythago Wood*;
>> Ursula K. Le Guin, *The Word For World is Forest*

# ISAAC ASIMOV (1920–92) USA

## I, ROBOT (1950)

One of the most consistently recurring motifs in SF has been the idea of artificial intelligence and thinking machines, and it was particularly prevalent in the decade and a half immediately after the Second World War. The classic 1940s' vision of the robot (although the stories were not published in book form until 1950, they had mostly appeared in SF magazines in the previous decade) is that of Isaac Asimov. Built around the famous Three Laws of Robotics, the stories collected in *I, Robot* did much to shape popular notions of what a robot might be and it is difficult to over-estimate their influence. Although the three laws were created by Asimov in close collaboration with *Astounding* editor ➤➤ John W. Campbell, it was Asimov who used them to most memorable effect. The nine stories in *I, Robot*, self-contained but tied together by the character of Susan Calvin, a robopsychologist working for the company which first manufactured the thinking machines, explore the consequences and implications of the laws when humans and robots interact. Through the stories Asimov not only builds up a gripping fictional history of the development of robotics from the late 20th century to the late 21st century but also sets out the logical and moral dilemmas that face both humans and robots as machine intelligence grows more powerful. In one story a robot on a space station, after logically deducing the existence of a deity, decides to serve God rather than man; in another a telepathic robot struggles to reconcile contradictory interpretations of the Laws and self-destructs when it finds it impossible to do so. Asimov's inventive stories, ranging in tone from darkly dystopian to humorous, examine questions about the dividing line between man and machine that have always intrigued SF writers.

📽 **Film version:** *I, Robot* (2004)

📚 **Read on**

*The Rest of the Robots*, *The Caves of Steel*, *The Naked Sun*
Artificial men: ➤➤ Barrington J. Bayley, *The Soul of a Robot*; Josef and Karel Capek *R.U.R.* (see Glossary: Robot); Sheila MacLeod, *Xanthe and the Robots*; ➤➤ Robert Silverberg, *Tower of Glass*; ➤➤ Jack Williamson, *The Humanoids*

# FOUNDATION (1953)

Asimov's *Foundation* trilogy, of which this is the first volume, is set far in the future when much of the known universe is united in a peaceful and largely benevolent galactic empire. Hari Seldon, a professor of psychohistory (statistical and psychological prediction of the future), foresees a disastrous era of war and anarchy in the empire to come, and establishes two Foundations on the galaxy's edge, apparently dedicated to safeguarding civilized knowledge until it is again required. This first volume concentrates on the first Foundation, allowing readers to watch its history unfold over more than a century in a series of snapshots from the passing decades. More of Seldon's long-term plans are revealed, years after his death. The influence of the Foundation begins to spread from the planet on which it was originally established to neighbouring worlds. Through the power of religion and trade, the seeds of a new civilization in waiting are planted.

Originally published in instalments in ›› John W. Campbell's *Astounding* magazine (which explains the episodic structure of the books), the Foundation trilogy is a massively ambitious attempt to map out the decline and eventual resurrection of an entire galaxy-wide civilization. Working on such a vast canvas, Asimov has little opportunity (or indeed inclination) to make use of subtlety of characterization or carefully nuanced plotting but this scarcely matters. In *Foundation*, he is not concerned with the ordinary and the everyday but with the large-scale workings of history and destiny. The grandeur of his imagination as he allows it the scope to play with the rise and fall of empires remains impressive more than fifty years after the books were first published. In later life Asimov returned to the Foundation universe to write a series of sequels. All are disappointing when compared to the epic vision of the original novels, written when the concept was fresh in Asimov's mind.

## ⮂ Read on

*Foundation and Empire*, *Second Foundation* (the other two volumes in the original *Foundation* trilogy)
Imperial explorations: ⮞ John Brunner, **Interstellar Empire**; ⮞ Arthur C. Clarke, *Imperial Earth*; Keith Laumer, *Retief*; ⮞ Ursula K. Le Guin, *Worlds of Exile and Illusion*; Dan Simmons, *Hyperion*

# J.G. BALLARD (b. 1930) UK

## THE DROWNED WORLD (1962)

In the mid-21st century an ecological disaster has struck the world. Temperatures have risen, the polar ice caps have melted and much of the Earth has been flooded. Only around the poles is civilization now possible. London has sunk beneath the waters and is at the centre of a vast swamp where life is much as it was in the Triassic Age. An expedition heads southwards from the Arctic to study the flora and fauna of this new world. One of the expedition members is a scientist named Robert Kerans. Amid the lush swamplands and hidden monuments of a drowned London, Kerans begins to experience strange dreams. Just as the Earth has regressed to a past state, so too Kerans seems to be making a psychic descent into prehistory. Left in the primal lagoons covering the city when the expedition heads back north, Kerans and two colleagues begin to respond to the deep, atavistic urges that are calling to them from the surreal landscape but they are interrupted by the arrival of Strangman, a dandified pirate with a cohort of violent henchmen intent on plundering the drowned world.

Ballard's fascination with the exploration of inner space and with plumbing the psychic depths, so unusual and liberating in the SF of the early 1960s, is most brilliantly revealed in *The Drowned World*. His prescience in describing a world transformed by environmental catastrophe may seem all the greater as the years pass but the strength of the novel lies not so much in this as in the voluptuous power with which he conjures up his vision of a primeval landscape and its effects on those who enter it. *The Drowned World* is a short novel but it is one that provides a startling and memorable perspective on the conscious and subconscious mind.

### ☙ Read on

*The Terminal Beach*, *The Drought*

Not with a Bang: ➤➤ Brian Aldiss, *Greybeard*; Anna Kavan, *Ice*; Adam Roberts, *The Snow*

## SUPER-CANNES (2000)

It is five minutes into the future or possibly the present. The resorts of the French Riviera are becoming studded with corporate office enclaves where the spreadsheet or R&D spec is king. One such antiseptic utopia of snowy concrete, flawless plate glass and immaculate though quiet leisure-retail complexes is Eden-Olympia, a blue-chip haven in the environs of what is known as Super-Cannes. Recuperating after a minor light aircraft accident, aviation publisher Paul Sinclair accompanies his paediatrician wife to Eden-Olympia: Jane's new appointment sees her replacing an ex-colleague who unaccountably gunned down seven local executives before shooting himself. Repelled yet intrigued by bluff, burly psychologist Wilder Penrose, the would-be caretaker of Eden-Olympia's hollow soul, Paul decides to investigate the mystery of the assassinations only to discover that behind the serene blandness of the colony lies a disturbing new social development. For where there is apparent clinical calm, a new kind of cathartic brutality is arising from a most unexpected source.

Echoing his early collection *Vermillion Sands*, *Super-Cannes* might be described as the second volume of a thematic tetralogy Ballard has produced recently (including *Cocaine Nights*, *Millennium People* and *Kingdom Come*), focusing on the effects of excessive luxury upon the middle classes. There are similarities between these books and his savage 1970s' urban series (*Crash*, *Concrete Island* and *High Rise*), as both sequences push the envelope of contemporary psychopathology with bullseye observations singularly relevant to their times. While hardcore Ballardians may rightly claim that the author will never produce a work more extreme than the epochal road-accident fetishism of *Crash*, his recent imagery is seductively subtle while his world-class prose has never been better.

Although Ballard has only produced one pure SF novel since the late sixties (*Hello America*), *Super-Cannes* is a masterful speculation in social science that can arguably be claimed for the genre. Alongside >> Dick and >> Priest, Ballard has done more to make us consider how (post)modernity has altered our consciousness. His significance as a cultural icon is mirrored by the success of slipstream novels like *American Psycho* and *Fight Club* where reality is what the protagonists say it is.

### ⬆ Read on

Mark Adlard, *Interface*; Martin Bax, *The Hospital Ship*; ›› William Gibson, *Pattern Recognition*; ›› Christopher Priest, *The Quiet Woman*; ›› Robert Silverberg, *To Live Again*

# IAIN M. BANKS (b. 1954) UK

## THE PLAYER OF GAMES (1988)

Nearly all of Banks's science fiction works are set in the seemingly utopian society of the far future he calls the Culture, a vast galaxy-wide civilization in which man and machine live in symbiotic harmony and individuals are allowed the time and the opportunity to develop their every talent and indulge their every desire. Nearly all of his plots begin at the point where apparent utopia either begins to break down or encounters less admirable societies. The central character of *The Player of Games* is Jernau Gurgeh, a man from the Culture whose entire life revolves around the playing of strategy games. In a society where leisure and recreation are so important, Gurgeh's expertise is valued and he is a famous and honoured man. He is also a dissatisfied man who feels that there should be more than endless comfort and privilege in his life. When the opportunity arises to take part in perhaps the greatest game in the universe, Gurgeh seizes it. As it expands, the Culture constantly comes into contact with other, less advanced societies. One of these is the Empire. The Empire is a society entirely founded on the playing of an elaborate war game. Success or failure in the game dictates each individual's position in the hierarchy. The greatest of all players becomes Emperor. Gurgeh journeys to the Empire to play as a guest in the game and succeeds beyond everyone's expectations. As he progresses further and further through the Empire's elaborate tournament, the dangers to his well-being grow and he learns more and more about the brutal realities that underpin the Empire's apparent civilization.

Banks is well known as a mainstream novelist (his first book, *The Wasp Factory*, remains controversial more than twenty years after publication) but his science fiction is also integral to his work as a writer and is clearly important to Banks himself. Within the vast, imaginative universe he has created in the Culture, he is able to tell stories which play wittily with ideas and concepts that he would struggle to incorporate in his non-SF fiction.

## ⮒ **Read on**

Other Culture novels: *Consider Phlebas*, *Use of Weapons*, *Excession*

Life's a gamble: ➤➤ Barrington J. Bayley, *The Grand Wheel*; ➤➤ Philip K. Dick, *Solar Lottery*; ➤➤ Barry N. Malzberg, *Tactics of Conquest*; ➤➤ Frederik Pohl and C.M. Kornbluth, *Gladiator at Law*; ➤➤ Ian Watson, *Queenmagic Kingmagic*

# STEPHEN BAXTER (b. 1957) UK

## MOONSEED (1998)

Opening with a snapshot from a fictional Apollo 18 landing on the moon and jumping swiftly to the awesome explosion of Venus in the night sky thirty years later, Stephen Baxter's novel of disaster and destruction starts (literally) with a bang and then moves progressively towards ever more Earth-threatening catastrophes. Henry Meacher is a geologist who travels to Edinburgh to investigate moon rock collected years earlier in the Apollo mission. Dust samples from the moon rock escape the laboratory and fall on the extinct volcano in the heart of the city. Soon the volcano is extinct no longer and the 'moonseed', its effects spreading rapidly, threatens Earth with the same explosive end as Venus. A race is on to save humanity and the only hope seems to lie in a mass evacuation to the moon. Neglected space technology has to be quickly revived to ensure a future for the survivors of the ongoing disaster.

Baxter, a graduate in mathematics and engineering, is one of the leading exponents of contemporary hard SF. His doomsday scenario in *Moonseed* is worked out with a strict adherence to scientific possibility and the practicality of the desperate attempts to leave a stricken Earth are described with a loving attention to detail and plausibility. Yet Baxter never neglects the storytelling essentials required to maintain the reader's interest. His plotting is cleverly organized to maximize the tension as the countdown to destruction continues and his characters, especially the flawed but credible Meacher, ring true. Baxter is a versatile and imaginative writer, whose other books range from epic future sagas spanning millions of years (the Xeelee sequence) to a sequel to ▶▶ H.G. Wells's *The Time Machine* (*The Time Ships*), but *Moonseed*, a bravura combination of thriller and hard SF, is perhaps his finest work.

### 🕮 Read on

*Ring, Titan, Evolution*
Astronauts: Ben Bova, *Privateers*; ▶▶ Samuel R. Delany, *Aye, and Gomorrah*; Nigel Kneale, *Quatermass II*; ▶▶ Larry Niven with Jerry Pournelle and Michael Flynn, *Fallen Angels*; ▶▶ Norman Spinrad, *Russian Spring*

# BARRINGTON J. BAYLEY (b. 1937) UK

## THE GARMENTS OF CAEN (1976)

In the Ziode Cluster, tailoring is a mundane occupation that ensures Peder Forbath remains a man of slender means, insignificant to the rest of society. But in Caen, a neighbouring galactic spiral arm, clothes are more than mere vestments, they are a way of life, encompassing not only a human being's philosophy but expanding his supernormal potential to boot. While the garments of Caen are illegal in the conservative Ziode, Forbath longs to elevate tailoring to its highest potential and become known as a Sartorial, the designation tailors enjoy in the culture next door. Falling in with foppish liqueur-sipping chancer Realto

Maast, Forbath participates in an illegal salvage mission on a frontier planet, raiding a wrecked cargo ship which contains a stash of Caenic couture that the duo will fence on the black market. But unknown to the villainous Maast, Peder has kept the prize of the haul for himself, a legendary Franchonard suit, one of only five in existence, much prized even in vogueish Caen. Soon Forbath finds his personality and fortunes transformed by his enigmatic garb, but Maast has learned of the deception and initiates a pursuit that leads to a galactic odyssey in which the clothes really do make the man.

Colourful, fast-moving and witty, *The Garments of Caen* is typical of Barry Bayley's inventive approach to traditional SF. With engaging characters and a vivid prose style that has an affinity with that of ›› Alfred Bester, ›› M. John Harrison and his friend ›› Michael Moorcock, Bayley is one of the most vital and entertaining of British writers, tackling perennial subjects such as space opera, time travel, robots and aliens in a refreshing manner that leaves the majority of genre SF authors standing. Although the book we've selected here is one of his most playful works, Bayley is equally at home with darker themes due to his affiliations with the British New Wave. We strongly recommend his novels to jaded readers looking for surprising takes on themes other writers have worn thin with overuse.

### ≋ Read on

*The Great Hydration, The Sinners of Erspia, The Zen Gun*
›› Michael Moorcock, *The Blood Red Game*; ›› M. John Harrison, *The Machine in Shaft Ten*

# GREG BEAR (b. 1951) USA

## BLOOD MUSIC (1985)

Many SF novels take as their subject the confrontation between man and alien. Usually the alien is out there – in the far reaches of space or on a distant planet. In *Blood Music*, almost more terrifyingly, the alien is within. In the last twenty-five years biology has replaced physics as the science that both promises us most and threatens us most, and SF has not been slow to take up the themes that DNA and genetic engineering have offered. *Blood Music* is one of the earliest and finest works of fiction to bring together the new biology and the old SF theme of the alien. Vergil Ulam is a maverick scientist who is sacked from the laboratory in which he has been carrying out cutting-edge experiments in cell biology. In order to continue with the work he has been doing, he injects his experimental cells into his own bloodstream. However, the cells have their own intelligence and, lodged within Ulam's body, they begin to evolve and mutate until they have taken it over and reworked his mind and consciousness for their benefit. Not only is Ulam now a vehicle for the cell intelligence but he is also highly infectious. The blood and brain plague he has unleashed is about to spread through humanity. Only a few people seem to carry an immunity to the mutating cells but they can do little to halt a process which is changing life and consciousness irreversibly.

Carrying echoes of ideas that have been present in SF since it began (the Frankenstein story of the hubristic scientist losing control of his own creation is an obvious influence), *Blood Music* is also a masterly fictional embodiment of much more contemporary debates. As genetic engineering and the possibilities of downloading consciousness to machines beckon us towards a post-human or transhuman future, Bear's engrossing novel remains essential reading.

🐢 **Read on**
*Queen of Angels, Darwin's Radio*
1980s American SF: David Brin, *Earth*; George Alec Effinger, *When Gravity Fails*; >> Kim Stanley Robinson, *A Memory of Whiteness*

# GREGORY BENFORD (b. 1941) USA

## TIMESCAPE (1980)

It is 1962. In the physics department at the University of California, Dr Gordon Bernstein is working on an experiment to measure nuclear resonance in a chemical compound. What should be a smooth piece of research is being affected by interference recorded by the monitoring apparatus. Establishing that the rogue data is no equipment problem, Bernstein realizes that the experiment is picking up a signal in Morse. Despite pressure from his academic peers to explain away the strange phenomenon in a manner acceptable to the scientific establishment, Bernstein secretly passes the data to a biochemist for interpretation. Ostracized by the academic community, Bernstein develops a startling new theory that will change physics, make his name and possibly alter the future. At Cambridge University in 1998 another scientist is attempting to utilize faster-than-light particles known as tachyons to send a message back to 1962 that could prevent the environmental collapse that threatens his world.

*Timescape* is the perfect answer to the misconceived argument that scientists cannot write excellent novels and it is one of the finest depictions of academic life in fiction. Benford is Professor of Physics at the University of California and his work has been acclaimed by both hard SF writers and literary figures such as ›› Anthony Burgess and ›› M. John Harrison. *Timescape* is scientifically accurate when it deals with contemporary theories about time. Smoothly written in a realistic style, it is packed with superbly realized characters of both sexes, including Peterson, the coolly calculating womanizer from the World Council of 1998, Penny, Bernstein's spiky, proto-hippy girlfriend and the awkward, tenacious Bernstein himself. No in-depth knowledge of physics is necessary to enjoy *Timescape*, but it is a marvellous book to pick up after putting your Stephen Hawking paperback down.

## ᘓ Read on

*If the Stars are Gods* (with Gordon Eklund), *The Heart of the Comet* (with David Brin)
Physics: ›› Isaac Asimov, *The Gods Themselves*; Poul Anderson, *Tau Zero*; Hal Clement, *Mission of Gravity*

# ALFRED BESTER (1913–87) USA

## THE DEMOLISHED MAN (1952)

Ben Reich is the volatile, power-hungry head of the Monarch Corporation, a multiplanetary company that is one of the most voracious business empires in the solar system. Haunted by a recurrent, violent nightmare of a faceless man, Reich seeks the help of a telepathic psychiatrist. Realizing that the only means to banish the dreams is to rid himself of business rival D'Courtney, Reich sets himself the objective of killing his fiscal arch-enemy. But in a world filled with 'Peepers', ESPer police who can read any mind, no man has got away with murder for decades. Disguising his homicidal intent by endlessly repeating a specially written mnemonic jingle in his head, Reich embarks on his atavistic purpose that could bestow upon him the ultimate sentence: demolition.

Lightning-paced, hard and glittering like the multiple facets of a cut diamond, *The Demolished Man* was not only Bester's first novel but also the first recipient of the Hugo Award for Best Novel. Having worked on newspaper comic strips, radio serials and short stories, Bester's disciplined, taut prose had no equal in the early fifties and this novel (published in *Galaxy*) raised the bar for writers wishing to escape the strictures ›› John W. Campbell had imposed upon magazine SF and create a fresh species of increasingly literate, socially aware speculations. Alongside his quicksilver plotting, razor-edged characters and enough energy to fuel a particle accelerator, Bester employed innovative techniques (such as using typographic layouts borrowed from concrete poetry in order to represent the mental conversations of Telepaths). The vibrant word-painting he brought to SF inspired future mavericks such as >> Delany, >> Ellison, >> Moorcock and >> Gibson, all of whom strove to further the modernist literary qualities of the genre. The best was yet to come: sublime short stories (the very best of which are collected in *Virtual Unreality*, which many believe are the greatest in the history of genre SF) appeared throughout the fifties alongside Bester's next novel (*The Stars My Destination*), a landmark work that outstrips even the senses-shattering genius of *The Demolished Man*, a book which none the less remains one of the most exhilarating rides SF has ever offered.

### ➰ Read on

*Galaxy* magazine doyens: Damon Knight, *In Deep*; Fritz Leiber, *The Big Time*; Edson McCann (>> Frederik Pohl and Lester Del Rey), *Preferred Risk*; Clifford Simak, *Ring Around the Sun*; >> Robert Sheckley, *Untouched by Human Hands*


## THE STARS MY DESTINATION (aka TIGER! TIGER!)
(1956)

Gulliver Foyle is the sole survivor aboard a wrecked spaceship who seems destined to die alone in the emptiness of space when his distress signals are ignored by another vessel, the *Vorga*. However, Gully succeeds in navigating his crippled ship to the Sargasso Asteroid, an isolated space outpost where the inhabitants have reverted to tribal savagery, and eventually escapes back to Earth where he starts his campaign of vengeance against the crew members of the *Vorga*. Slowly, driven by his overwhelming desire for revenge, he moves closer and closer to Presteign of Presteign, the fabulously wealthy owner of the

*Vorga*, who has his own reasons for wanting a confrontation with Gully.

*The Stars My Destination* is a breathtaking narrative that scarcely ever pauses for a moment as its implacable anti-hero relentlessly pursues his goals. On the future Earth that Bester imagines, a man named Jaunte has discovered a means of mental transportation which takes his name. Jaunting is at the heart of *The Stars My Destination*, just as ESP fuels the plot of *The Demolished Man*, and the plot moves with the same speed as jaunters propelling themselves through space.

The sheer prodigality of Bester's inventiveness is remarkable. Ideas which another writer would have stretched out to support an entire novel, Bester recklessly and exhilaratingly throws away in the space of a paragraph or two. The book is dominated by the driven outsider Gully Foyle, one of the most unforgettable characters in all of SF, but it is also a vehicle for its author's pyrotechnic displays of imagination. ▶▶ Harlan Ellison once said that, 'Bester was the mountain, all the rest of us merely climbers toward that peak', and *The Stars My Destination*, together with *The Demolished Man*, reveals just why other writers continue to admire him so much.

## 📖 Read on

*Golem 100, The Dark Side of the Earth*
Poul Anderson, *Brain Wave*; ▶▶ James Blish, *Jack of Eagles*; ▶▶ John Brunner, *Telepathist*; Charles Harness, *The Paradox Men*

# MICHAEL BISHOP (b. 1945) USA

## ANCIENT OF DAYS (1985)

When restaurant owner Paul Lloyd takes a phone call from his commercial artist ex-wife RuthClaire telling him that a strange pint-sized being is sitting in a tree in her garden, he readily offers assistance. Despite the mild cynicism Paul employs to dampen his continued attachment to RuthClaire, he has to admit she is correct: the mysterious visitor is a specimen of *Homo Habilis*, one of mankind's ancestors thought to be extinct for a million years. But what is 'Handy Man' doing in contemporary Bible Belt USA? To Paul's dismay, RuthClaire coaxes 'Adam' into the couple's former shared home and shortly the Habiline is sharing her bed. Stifling his jealousy, Paul's sidelined role in the ménage shifts when the world's scientific and tabloid press discover Adam, and the local Ku Klux Klan takes an unhealthy interest in the protohuman's racial provenance. Just as RuthClaire accepts a commission to paint a tableware set depicting the genealogical tree of the family Hominidae, Adam is forced to defend himself in a manner that will have tragic consequences.

Michael Bishop emerged as a leading writer of anthropological SF in the seventies, displaying his interest in human behaviour in a number of novels set on other planets. Displaying an ease with social comedy written in a persuasive mainstream style, *Ancient of Days* tackles the question of how we define ourselves in a warm, dignified manner. Deftly ensuring that the absurd elements of Adam's spiritual trans-formation from nut-nibbler to amateur theologian never descend into slapstick, this gently amusing yet thoughtful book also conjures considerable sympathy for the ousted Paul without descending into mawkishness. Bishop also wrote the first SF novel about >> Philip K. Dick, the gripping homage *The Secret Ascension* (aka *Philip K. Dick is Dead, Alas*). Far more obscure than he deserves, Bishop provides an humanistic foil to the hi-tech attractions of the postmodern, cyberpunk and new radical hard SF that have dominated the genre for the past two decades.

### ᕫ Read on

*Count Geiger's Blues*
Are we not men? (SF goes ape): Paddy Chayefsky, *Altered States*; >> Philip José Farmer, *The Alley Man*; Jack London, *Before Adam*; Will Self, *Great Apes*

# JAMES BLISH (1921–75) USA

## A CASE OF CONSCIENCE (1958)

On the planet Lithia a small team of human scientists is working to assess the alien world's suitability as a port of call for space travellers from Earth. One of the scientists, a biologist named Ramon Ruiz-Sanchez, is also a Jesuit priest and, as he studies Lithia and its dominant species, an intelligent reptile twice the height of humans, he begins to ask himself questions about the nature of Lithian society. Is Lithia the paradise it seems, a place where perfect peace and contentment reign, or is it something entirely different? Is it, in fact, a planet created by the devil specifically to tempt man with a vision of an unfallen world? As the narrative shifts back to Earth and follows the growth to adulthood of Egtverchi, a young Lithian who has been sent back with the exploratory team, Ruiz-Sanchez's doubts and crises of conscience only grow worse until he is impelled towards a dramatic and irreversible resolution of them.

Nearly fifty years after its first publication, *A Case of Conscience* remains one of the most unusual and thought-provoking SF novels ever written. Blish gives no indication that we are supposed to assume that the Jesuit's beliefs about Lithia are correct. His interest is not in religion as such but in the moral dilemmas that confrontation with 'otherness' produces. The conclusions at which Ruiz-Sanchez arrives are not those likely to be reached by most readers but the genuine agonies of conscience he suffers are brilliantly evoked. In his later career, Blish worked largely on *Star Trek* novelizations but his original fiction, from *Cities in Flight* (a collection of linked stories in which tramp cities, plucked from their terrestrial settings, wander the universe) to *A Case of Conscience*, makes philosophically stimulating and imaginative reading.

## ❧ Read on

*Dr Mirabilis*, *Black Easter/The Day After Judgement* (Blish's thematic sequels to *A Case of Conscience* are a stand-alone novel and two interconnected novels that are known collectively alongside *Conscience* as the *After Such Knowledge* trilogy)
>> Philip José Farmer, *Father to the Stars*; R.A. Lafferty, *Past Master*; Mary Doria Russell, *The Sparrow*

# RAY BRADBURY (b. 1920) USA

## THE MARTIAN CHRONICLES (aka THE SILVER LOCUSTS) (1950)

It is Rocket Summer in Ohio. Everyone talks about the first manned expedition to Mars, seduced by the majesty of the escapade. We follow the failures of their first missions, learn of the shifting physical and psionic character of the child-like yet calculating Martians as the latter realize that the invaders from the third planet are not going to relinquish their dreams of dominion easily. Reading like the steps of a swooning dance that so often ends in shadow, the book shows the Martians advancing in their silver masks as death stalks the sons of Earth. Like virtually all the genre SF novels written before the mid-fifties, *The Martian Chronicles* comprised a sequence of linked stories that were published in the pulps. But *The Martian Chronicles* was not a serial, but a collection of vignettes. Freed from the convention of a narrative that focused on a handful of characters, this approach allowed Bradbury to exploit fresh angles on (and startling insights into) the diverse aspects of men and Martians with each successive tale. The result is a singularly compulsive book that expertly explores humanity's naïve expectations of the alien and the thoughtless cruelty of our pre-dispositions as conquerors. The author also expresses the strangeness of the inscrutable Martians with a lyrical gift that still fascinates readers today.

Bradbury's early history as a deft exponent of crime, fantasy and horror stories ensured that by the late forties he was a virtuoso of shock, a quality that he matched with a homely charm that outstripped all his contemporaries. *The Martian Chronicles* saw the flowering of Bradbury's mature, poetic style that won him boundless praise from mainstream critics, resulting in a career as one of the definitive short story writers for the slick magazines. *The Martian Chronicles* is a flawless introduction to the planetary romance for anyone who has never read SF and it continues to be luxuriated in by those whose shelves groan with the weight of gaudy paperbacks. Fitting successor to the Martian dreams of ›› Edgar Rice Burroughs, Leigh Brackett and ›› C.L. Moore, it remains the greatest novel ever published about the red planet.

◻ **TV Series**: *The Martian Chronicles* (1980)

≋ **Read on**
*The October Country, The Illustrated Man* (both volumes of short stories)
Life on Mars: ›› D.G. Compton, *Farewell, Earth's Bliss*; ›› Philip K. Dick, *Martian Time-Slip*; Ian MacDonald, *Desolation Road*; Lewis Shiner, *Frontera*; Stanley G. Weinbaum, *A Martian Odyssey*

## FAHRENHEIT 451 (1953)

Guy Montag is a fireman in 24th-century America. Unlike firemen today, Montag's job is not to extinguish fires but to set them. Specifically, he is required to burn books and the houses of those who own them. (Bradbury's title refers to the temperature at which the paper used in books catches fire.) In the oppressive society of the future, books and the potentially liberating knowledge they contain are illegal. At first happy in his work and his life, Montag begins to question the values of his world. His friendship with the teenage Clarisse McClellan, whose openness to experience and to nature stands in contrast to his wife's brain-numbing addiction to interactive television and tranquilizers, unsettles him. So too does the inexplicable behaviour of an old woman to whose house he is called. Rather than abandon her books, she burns with them. What power can books have that some people are prepared to die rather than relinquish them? Not for the first time, Montag steals a book from one of the collections he is supposed to burn. When he hears of the death of Clarisse in a car accident, he falls even further into depression and confusion. As the novel progresses, the fireman is torn between his old life, represented by his boss Captain Beatty, and a new, clandestine world of books and ideas, personified by the retired Professor Faber. Finally, after a climactic confrontation with Beatty, Montag faces a choice between conformity and freedom. He chooses freedom and escapes to join an outlaw group of intellectuals who have memorized the world's great books in order to preserve them for the future. Beginning life as a short story called 'The Fireman' which was published in *Galaxy Science Fiction* in 1951, *Fahrenheit 451* appeared in its extended, book form two years later. Imbued with Bradbury's old-fashioned humanism and decency, and written in his characteristic prose, which can effortlessly blend the everyday with the poetic, the novel remains one of the finest achievements of traditional 1950s' SF.

**◄ Film version:** Fahrenheit 451 (1967)

**◈ Read on**

Dystopia USA: **▸▸** Thomas M. Disch, *334*; David Karp, *One*; C.M. Kornbluth, *The Syndic*; Ayn Rand, *Atlas Shrugged*; Mack Reynolds, *Commune 2000 A.D.*

# JOHN BRUNNER (1934–95) UK

## THE SHEEP LOOK UP (1972)

Brunner published his first SF novel when he was seventeen and was a remarkably prolific author from the 1950s to the 1990s but he is likely to be best remembered for a handful of novels he produced in the late 1960s and early 1970s. *The Shockwave Rider*, with its prescient vision of computer networks and viruses, is often cited as a forerunner of cyberpunk. *Stand on Zanzibar* not only tackles the theme of over-population unflinchingly but it does so in a marvellously ambitious array of styles and techniques that owes more to major American modernist fiction like John Dos Passos's *USA* than it does to the average SF novel. *Stand on Zanzibar* has always been Brunner's most highly acclaimed book (it won both the Hugo award and the inaugural BSFA award in the year it was published) but *The Sheep Look Up*, published three years later, is an equally challenging dystopia which took the then unfashionable subject of environmental degradation and conjured from it a dark yet gripping vision of a dying world.

Water shortages cause chaos, climate change is devastating the planet and new diseases have emerged to plague humanity. At the heart of Brunner's story is the environmentalist Austin Train, whose writings cataloguing our abuse of the Earth have become bestsellers, and who has become the unwitting (and sometimes unwilling) inspiration for thousands of 'Trainites' across the USA. But, like *Stand on Zanzibar*, *The Sheep Look Up* is a portrait of a sick world painted on a giant canvas. The narrative branches out in dozens of directions; an array of characters, from millionaires and muckraking journalists to TV stars and political radicals, jostles for the reader's attention; and Brunner makes use of every means he can devise (news reports from around the world, transcripts of interviews, advertizements) in order to tell his story of a planet racing towards its doom. Angry and inspired, Brunner's novel has even more relevance today than it had when it was first published.

### ⮬ Read on

*Stand on Zanzibar, The Jagged Orbit, The Shockwave Rider*
**>>** Thomas M. Disch (ed.), *The Ruins of Earth*; Charles Platt, *Garbage World*

# ALGIS BUDRYS (b. 1931) USA

## ROGUE MOON (1960)

An alien artefact has been discovered on the moon. The maze-like object can only be explored by the transmission of bodily duplicates of individuals to the moon. The duplicate beings die, usually within seconds of entering the object, but, before they die, each can maintain telepathic contact with his original on Earth. The originals experience the deaths of their other selves and the ordeal drives them insane. Only one man seems to be immune to the traumatic effects of witnessing the death of his duplicated self. Al Barker, a confirmed risk-taker and devotee of extreme sports, is repeatedly duplicated. Time and again his duplicate travels to the moon, enters the maze and dies. But each journey brings a little more information about the strange artefact back to Earth and eventually the maze is mapped. Barker's bloody-minded, perverse courage and the faith in science of Edward Hawks, the man who created the machinery to transmit the duplicates to the moon, have been justified.

Algis Budrys was born in East Prussia in 1931 and came to America with his Lithuanian family when he was five years old. He has not been a prolific writer and he is another of those many SF authors whose best work can arguably be found in their short stories rather than in their longer fiction. However, *Rogue Moon* remains an utterly compelling novel, as gripping in its analysis of the complicated psychologies of its central characters as it is in the unfolding of its plot. The image of the enigmatic alien artefact, the purpose of which is never discovered, the deranged determination with which Barker resurrects himself over and over again and Hawks's indomitable belief in the power of the human mind to overcome all obstacles remain with the reader long after the book is finished.

### ⪾ Read on
*Michaelmas*, *The Furious Future* (short stories)
Trapped: ≫ Harlan Ellison, *I Have No Mouth and I Must Scream*; ≫ Philip José Farmer, *The Green Odyssey*; ≫ Robert Silverberg, *Shadrach in the Furnace*; ≫ A.E. Van Vogt, *The Mind Cage*

# ANTHONY BURGESS (1917–93) UK

## A CLOCKWORK ORANGE (1962)

In a near future, near totalitarian society, teenage gangs run rampant. Amphetamine and psychedelic drugs fuel their indulgence in recreational sex and violence. The novel is narrated by Alex, one of the gang members, in the distinctive argot used by the teenagers, derived largely from corrupted Russian words and known as 'nadsat'. Alex is a paradoxical anti-hero. He is a thug whose ideas of a good time involve rape and blood-letting but he is also a passionate enthusiast for classical music, especially the works of Beethoven. After breaking into a house and beating an old man to death, Alex is arrested and forced to become the subject of an experiment in advanced aversion therapy. Films of violence and torture are shown to him while drugs induce sickness and vomiting. With his favourite Ludwig van playing as background music, Alex learns a connection between violence and his own physical discomfort. When he emerges from the experiment, he is apparently cured of his taste for antisocial behaviour but he has also lost his delight in Beethoven.

Burgess's arguments in favour of free will and his distaste for the kind of conditioning inflicted on Alex are clear enough but the strength of *A Clockwork Orange* lies not so much in any 'message' its narrative may contain but in the extraordinary inventiveness and energy of the language in which it is written. In later years, the multi-talented Burgess, who published many other novels, claimed not to care for *A Clockwork Orange* and expressed regret that it seemed likely to be the book for which he would be best remembered. More than a decade after his death, it is still his best-known work by far, but Burgess's dislike of it seems difficult to understand. As a blackly comic vision of a violent future, written in language of startling originality, *A Clockwork Orange* remains one of the most memorable of all SF dystopias.

**Film version:** *A Clockwork Orange* (1971)

**Read on**

Euro-dystopia: ›› J.G. Ballard, *Kingdom Come*; ›› Michael Moorcock (with Hilary Bailey, uncredited), *The Black Corridor*; Derek Raymond, *A State of Denmark*; Tricia Sullivan, *Maul*; ›› H.G. Wells, *The Sleeper Awakes*

# EDGAR RICE BURROUGHS (1875–1950) USA

## A PRINCESS OF MARS (1912)

Pursued by Apaches in the wilds of Arizona, former confederate officer John Carter finds himself mysteriously transported to Barsoom, a planet carpeted with yellow moss that he recognizes as Mars. Although the lower Martian gravity gives Carter stupendous agility relative to his size, he is nevertheless snared by a giant, four-armed, green-skinned alien known as a Thark. Despite entering a near-deserted Martian citadel as a captive, Carter gradually wins the respect of the brutal yet honourable humanoids, developing telepathic powers and proving his mettle as a warrior in the arena. When a flotilla of mysterious airships appears above their city, the monstrous Tharks bring one down, capturing a copper-skinned, sable-maned woman of impeccable beauty – the delectable Dejah Thoris, Princess of Helium, mistress of an empire that has long been the nemesis of Carter's hosts....

The first of eleven books of Barsoom, this slender volume is *the* classic pulp vision of Mars: dead seas, oviparous aliens, strange customs and high adventure. Although the science in the book is negligible, its striking setting and bold use of fantasy elements have ensured that this landmark novel has the best claim to being the original Planetary Romance – its vivid colours and lively inventiveness, tinted with sharp heroism and discreet flashes of eroticism confirm it as the seminal work of the subgenre that developed in its wake. Even after decades of numerous imitations, it remains an unputdownable exploit with a cliffhanger finish that leaves the reader ravenous for more tales of Carter and Thoris. *Princess* was Edgar Rice Burroughs' first book, which was soon followed by *Tarzan of the Apes* and a host of other definitive SF and fantasy novels. Although as a literary stylist his work is closer in quality to that of Verne than Wells, Burroughs' mastery in creating noble yet savage heroes combined with a command of adventure narrative that rivals Conan Doyle made him one of the most important pioneers in the development of genre fiction.

## ☙ Read on

Other key ERB: *Tarzan of the Apes*, *The People That Time Forgot*, *The Gods of Mars* (sequel to *Princess*)

Burroughsian Planetary Romance: Leigh Brackett, *Sea Kings of Mars*;
➤➤ Philip José Farmer, *Two Hawks From Earth*; ➤➤ Jack Vance, *Big Planet*

## READONATHEME: HEROIC FANTASY

The finest sword and sorcery fiction beyond Tolkien

Poul Anderson, *The Broken Sword*
>>John Brunner, *The Compleat Traveller in Black*
Stephen Donaldson, *The Chronicles of Thomas Covenant*
E.R. Eddison, *The Worm Ouroboros*
John Gardner, *Grendel*
Robert E. Howard, *The Complete Chronicles of Conan*
>>Ursula K. Le Guin, *The Earthsea Quartet*
Fritz Leiber, *The First Book of Lankhmar*
Patricia McKillip, *The Riddle-Masters Game*
>>Michael Moorcock, *Elric of Melnibone*
Michael Shea, *The Incompleat Nifft*
Christopher Stasheff, *The Warlock in Spite of Himself*

# WILLIAM S. BURROUGHS (1914–97) USA

## THE TICKET THAT EXPLODED (1967)

Willy the Rat, heavy metal addict from Uranus; The Subliminal Kid;
Hamburger Mary; Mr Bradly Mr Martin. Members of the Nova Mob, a
cadre of extraterrestrial criminals from vile worlds. Their scam is to bribe

and con the control systems of planets they hit – easily corruptible governments and corporations, eager to turn a profit and/or wield power for its own sake. The Mob has loathsome appetites, exploiting their target planet to the max by draining its energies and deriving repulsive sexual kicks from the enslaved populace whom they manipulate through all manner of addictions. Working through politician and board director puppets, the Mob generate WMD conflicts, escaping into outer space before the planet goes 'nova' in thermonuclear war. An anti-organization called The Nova Police is fronted by Inspector J. Lee, a being dedicated to snapping antibiotic handcuffs on the aliens. When the Mob reaches Earth, cosmic alarms trigger and Lee (Burroughs himself) and his operatives materialize on primitive Terra, the inspector admitting he has never seen such fear and degradation.

Burroughs was magus of the Beats, a literary movement that inspired generations of underground nonconformists. Homosexual, dope fiend and SF reader, Burroughs' most celebrated book is *The Naked Lunch*, originally issued by legendary avant-garde/pornography publisher Olympia Press. Denounced as obscene by some and fêted as a masterpiece by others, this collection of sketches has been described as the first part of a trilogy. However, *The Naked Lunch* does not use the same basic narrative (described above) as *The Soft Machine*, *The Ticket That Exploded* and *Nova Express*, although it is thematically similar. The Nova Trilogy (which can be read in any order) also employs the radical 'cut-up' technique Burroughs is infamous for, whereas *The Naked Lunch* does not. Devised by surrealist painter Brion Gysin, these experiments involved Burroughs taking pages from books (including ❯❯ Henry Kuttner's *Fury*), magazines and newspapers then scissoring them into strips, creating new sentences. Startling juxtapositions and striking images sometimes resulted from these games, which Burroughs then incorporated into his SF, often creating dizzying effects of randomness and shamanic repetition. Although challenging for the reader, the finished text is extremely exciting once one grows familiar with this innovative approach. *The Ticket That Exploded* is the most avant-garde and rewarding of the trilogy.

As many readers try *The Naked Lunch* and never finish it, we recommend everyone read *Junky* (Burroughs' straightforward yet superb autobiographical novel about heroin addiction) first before tackling other Burroughs as this will familiarize them with the narcotics slang and countercultural scenarios the author uses throughout his work. The fundamental influence on the New Wave, Burroughs' amazing non-linear satires are essential reading for an understanding of contemporary literary SF.

## ᘓ Read on

Burroughsian New Wave: **>>** J.G. Ballard, *The Atrocity Exhibition*; Langdon Jones (ed.), *The New SF*; **>>** Michael Moorcock (ed), *New Worlds: An Anthology*

Hardboiled criminal futures: Curt Clark (Richard Stark), *Anarchaos*; Lester Del Rey, *Police Your Planet*

# PAT CADIGAN (b. 1953) USA

## SYNNERS (1991)

The next San Francisco earthquake has come and gone. Gabe Ludovic works in marketing for Diversifications Inc., an IT multinational producing medical implants. Routinely spending his time in virtual reality simulations with people he has never actually met, Gabe's career is on the slide and his marriage is breaking down as his wife's own success edges toward the apex of its bell curve. Even the AI housekeeper wired into the walls of his condo berates him for a lack of ambition that has kept him from producing computer art in his free time.

Gabe's rebellious teenage daughter Gina still has the aesthetic temperament her father squanders. She is a Synner, a computech-manipulating hacker adept at withdrawing images from the minds of performers and converting them into virtual reality software for others to experience. Gina's partner at EyeTraxx is Visual Mark, a youth with a natural genius for alternative rock videos, the VR medium the small company excels at. But EyeTraxx has been acquired by Diversifications Inc., who plan to utilize Visual Mark's skills to trial and sell implants that can involve the buyer in dreams synthesized from the subsconscious of others. But in the grey area where big business meets the outsider attitudes of these near-future EMO-metal kids, a struggle for freedom in the interface between human minds and corporate networks develops a third corner when mysterious computer viruses enter the fray.

Pat Cadigan's rightful claim to be the first lady of cyberpunk (the term was taken from the title of a story by Bruce Bethke and applied to the fledgling subgenre by editor-author Gardner Dozois) dates back to her story 'Rock On' appearing in ❯❯ Bruce Sterling's seminal *Mirrorshades* anthology. Although several other female writers have attempted cyberpunk writing with mixed results, Cadigan remains without serious competition, displaying a debt to ❯❯ Dick and a willingness to engage with plot complexity that outpaces her male contemporaries too. *Synners* is possibly the finest cyberpunk novel outside ❯❯ Gibson's oeuvre – its multitude of characters, convincing near-future scenarios and vertiginous multiple thread narrative creating a vividly realized designer vision of the day after the day after tomorrow.

### ≋ Read on
*Fools*
Cyberpunk aftermath: Bruce Bethke, *Rim*; Richard Kadrey, *Metrophage*; Jeff Noon, *Vurt*; Jack Womack, *Ambient*

# JOHN W. CAMPBELL JR (1910–71) USA

## THE BEST OF JOHN W. CAMPBELL (collected 1973)
Scientists at an Antarctic research station are surprised to discover an unexpected magnetic force indicated on their instruments. Their investigation leads to something uncanny encased deep in the polar ice: an immense object buried for 20 million years. The group deduces that the find must be from beyond Earth as one of its occupants managed to crawl out of the machine before it froze to death: a dwarfish being with three red eyes and blue vermiform hair. Excavating the

extraterrestrial from its wintry grave and returning to their camp, the men soon discover that their unique specimen is no longer inert but that it poses a greater threat to the planet than they could have imagined: a colonial creature whose every cell is an independent organism, it can assimilate and mimic any life-form perfectly. The group realize they can no longer trust their friends as any one of them could be *a thing*. It will take all of their inventiveness, resolve and desire to prove that man is master of the universe and to ensure they survive the onslaught of the invader and stop its progeny infecting the entire world.

'Who Goes There?' (1938) is one of five superb stories in this essential collection by *the* architect of modern genre SF. It has been filmed twice, the later version being more faithful to the original tale. Editor of *Astounding* from 1937 until his death, Campbell insisted that his writers worked hard at their craft, raising the bar for literary quality, scientific accuracy and disciplined extrapolation, ensuring the plot consequences of their ideas were worked out logically. In the late thirties Campbell discovered ➤➤ Asimov, ➤➤ Heinlein, ➤➤ Sturgeon and ➤➤ Van Vogt (among many others) and ushered in the Golden Age of pulp SF. His editorial policy moulded the genre until the early fifties and his influence remains prevalent even today. Barred from writing and selling to other publishers or even contributing stories to his own magazine by its owners, Campbell sacrificed his authorial career to *Astounding*. His stories are essential reading – exciting and well-executed, they provide vital insights into the approach of the most influential editor in the history of SF. Campbell's belief in man's intellect and *Übermensch* potential has led to some commentators labelling him as right-wing (an influence perhaps most prevalent on Heinlein and Van Vogt) but it would be fairer to say that his optimism and faith in mankind are typical of the trailblazing spirit of scientific discovery upon which SF ultimately depends for its inspiration.

**◀ Film versions**: *The Thing* aka *The Thing From Another World* (1951), *The Thing* (1982)

## ⮑ Read on

Astounding's Golden Age: **»** Isaac Asimov, *Nightfall*; **»** Robert A. Heinlein, *Methuselah's Children*; **»** Theodore Sturgeon, *Microcosmic God*; **»** A.E. Van Vogt, *The World of Null-A*; **»** Jack Williamson, *Seetee Ship*

---

### READONATHEME: BOOK OF THE FILM

Numerous SF novels and stories have been adapted for cinema or have inspired original screenplays. This listing identifies the literary sources of some (in)famous SF films:

THE BEAST FROM 20,000 FATHOMS: **»** Ray Bradbury, 'The Fog Horn' (From T*he Golden Apples of the Sun*)

DAMNATION ALLEY: **»** Roger Zelazny, *Damnation Alley*

THE DAY THE EARTH STOOD STILL: Harry Bates, 'Farewell to the Master' (uncollected, readable online at www.thenostalgia league.com)

DR STRANGELOVE: Peter George, *Red Alert*

THE FLY: George Langelaan, 'The Fly' (from *Out Of Time*)

IMPOSTOR: **»** Philip K. Dick, 'Impostor' (from *Second Variety*)

---

THE INCREDIBLE SHRINKING MAN: ›› Richard Matheson, *The Shrinking Man*

IT CAME FROM OUTER SPACE: ›› Ray Bradbury, 'The Meteor' (from *It Came From Outer Space*)

LIFEFORCE: Colin Wilson, *The Space Vampires*

LOGAN'S RUN: William F. Nolan and George Clayton Johnson, *Logan's Run*

MINORITY REPORT: ›› Philip K. Dick, 'Minority Report' (from *The Days of Perky Pat* aka *Minority Report*)

MYSTERIOUS ISLAND: ›› Jules Verne, *The Mysterious Island*

NEW ROSE HOTEL: ›› William Gibson, 'New Rose Hotel' (from *Burning Chrome*)

PAYCHECK: ›› Philip K. Dick, 'Paycheck' (from *Beyond Lies the Wub*)

PLANET OF THE APES: Pierre Boulle, *Monkey Planet* (aka *Planet of the Apes*)

THE PRESTIGE: ›› Christopher Priest, *The Prestige*

ROLLERBALL: William Harrison, 'Roller Ball Murder' (from *Rollerball*)

SCREAMERS: ›› Philip K. Dick, 'Second Variety' (from *Second Variety*)

THE TERMINATOR: ›› Harlan Ellison, 'Soldier' (from *From the Land of Fear*)

TOTAL RECALL: ›› Philip K. Dick, 'We Can Remember It For You Wholesale' (from *We Can Remember It For You Wholesale* aka *The Little Black Box*)

# ORSON SCOTT CARD (b. 1951) USA

## ENDER'S GAME (1985)

Two wars have been fought by humans against ant-like invaders from space. Neither war finished in conclusive victory and the world anxiously awaits an inevitable third invasion. In preparation for this, an elite corps of genius children is being trained to become Earth's secret weapon in the coming struggle. Isolated in a Battle School in space, the children endlessly play war games, devising strategies and techniques that will help them in the role they have been assigned. The star of the school is a young child named Ender Wiggin. When readers first meet him, Ender is only six years old but his precocious genius has been recognized by the authorities and his rigorous training has begun. Taken from his parents and family and starved of love and affection, Ender has no option but to become the self-reliant, swift-thinking and ruthless wargamer the world requires. As he scales the rungs of the training ladder at the school, he is closely observed by the powers that be, who have a particular destiny in mind for him.

*Ender's Game* does have its drawbacks. Unfortunately for British readers, the ant-like aliens are known as 'buggers'. Constant references to the 'bugger wars', 'defeating all buggers' and so on sound at first very odd – indeed risible – but it is more than worth persevering with the book to the point where they cease to do so. The novel is an adventure story of a self-sufficient hero, albeit one who is only a child, surviving in circumstances where all the world seems against him, but it also works as a sophisticated moral tale in which the martial virtues so often celebrated in American culture (and, indeed, in American SF) are examined and questioned. Orson Scott Card is a Mormon who has been a prolific writer of both SF and fantasy in the twenty years since the publication of *Ender's Game*. The story of Ender Wiggin continued along often surprising paths in several sequels but it is the first instalment in the saga which most successfully revealed Card's ability to combine exciting narrative with moral parable.

### 🥢 Read on

Sequels: *Speaker For the Dead*, *Xenocide*
Gifted children: ➤➤ Greg Bear, *Anvil of Stars*; Richard Cowper, *Kuldesak*; ➤➤ John Wyndham, *Chocky*

# ANGELA CARTER (1940–92) UK

## HEROES AND VILLAINS (1969)

Angela Carter's death from cancer in 1992 robbed modern English literature of one of its most original and inventive talents. All her books contained elements of fantasy and speculation but few of them can be convincingly claimed for science fiction. *Heroes and Villains* is one of them. It is set in a future world that has been devastated by nuclear disaster – although Carter places little emphasis on this and her interest is in the characters who populate the world rather than the events which brought it into being. Her central character, Marianne, lives in what is (almost literally) an ivory tower – an isolated bastion of literacy and technological know-how in a wild forest filled with

Barbarians, tattooed men and women who have reverted to tribal primitivism. Marianne's father is one of the Professors, the group that preserves the pre-holocaust heritage but, after his death, she escapes into the forest and joins forces with Jewel, a Barbarian leader whose vitality and virility both fascinates and appals her. In Jewel's company, she experiences the often brutal reality of life outside the confines of the ivory tower.

*Heroes and Villains* is a remarkable book which, even after several readings, remains open to endless interpretation and re-interpretation. On the one hand it is a baroque tale of the future, filled with fantasy and magic, in which the heroine is led from her sheltered world to a richer but more dangerous one. On the other, it is a fable of civilization meeting barbarism in which the sterile rationality of the Professors in their towers is seen as inadequate and constraining. Men and, more significantly, women need to confront the irrational and the primitive within them and to learn the value of imagination and mystery in their lives if they are to become their true selves.

## ☜ Read on

*The Infernal Desire Machines of Dr Hoffman*, *The Bloody Chamber*
Structural fabulation (self-conscious literary SF): Paul Auster, *In the Country of Last Things*; John Crowley, *Little Big*; Craig Kee Strete, *If All Else Fails*

# ARTHUR C. CLARKE (b. 1917) UK

## CHILDHOOD'S END (1953)

Sometime in the not too distant future, man is about to begin his own voyages into space when giant spaceships suddenly appear in the skies over the world's major cities. The Overlords have arrived. Unlike so many aliens in SF, these mighty beings, despite their appearance (unveiled in a brilliant revelatory moment about a third of the way through the book), are not out to destroy humanity but to redeem it. Under their tutelage mankind heads towards utopia. Poverty, crime and unhappiness become half-forgotten scourges of a time before the Overlords came. Science and rationality rule the world, as Clarke delights in describing his vision of what a sane society might be. But the children of this utopia are about to take one further evolutionary step. As they prepare to transcend previous human limits, the Overlords are again there to guide them.

When discussion turns to the predictive power of science fiction, Arthur C. Clarke's name is often the first to be mentioned. With his own scientific background (he studied physics and mathematics at the University of London), Clarke was, from the beginning, intent on providing his readers with convincing visions of what the future might hold. Yet today the novels and short stories of technological prescience seem less interesting than a book like *Childhood's End* with its suggestions of religious mysticism sheltering behind the science. Best-known now for his collaboration with Stanley Kubrick on the innovative 1968 movie *2001: A Space Odyssey*, which had its starting point in his story 'The Sentinel' and was later expanded into a novel, Clarke is no master prose stylist or ground-breaking original talent but he has proved one of the most long-lasting and influential exponents of a particular style of hard SF. *Childhood's End* is not typical of his work but it remains one of his finest achievements.

## ⮆ Read on
*The City and the Stars*, *The Deep Range*, *Songs of Distant Earth*
Sense of wonder: ⮞⮞ Stephen Baxter, *Ring*; Jack McDevitt, *The Engines of God*; ⮞⮞ Frederik Pohl, *Gateway*; Olaf Stapledon, *Last and First Men*; David Zindell, *Neverness*

# D.G. COMPTON (b. 1930) UK

## THE CONTINUOUS KATHERINE MORTENHOE (1974)
As a television reporter, Rod is used to treading the line between journalistic objectivity and vicarious involvement. Taking a new assignment on *The Human Destiny Show*, a top-rated reality programme that follows the stories of accident victims, the mentally ill and terminal cases, Rod agrees (for a large sum) to have radical microsurgery performed on his eyes for a new angle on the human tragedies the series covers: Rod will no longer be in front of the camera, he will be the camera. The latest subject of the series has absconded after signing a contract and taking the money, so Rod's assignment is to find her and gain her trust without revealing his true purpose while the audience

watches voyeuristically though the journalist's eyes. For Katherine Mortenhoe is a fortyish divorcee suffering from a fatal disease, a rarity in the world of tomorrow, and her decline towards an inevitable death will be compulsive viewing for an audience starved of traumatic catharsis. As Rod grows to know Katherine he finds many parallels with his own life – he too is estranged and separated from a partner who mistrusts the ethical compromises Rod's career has encouraged him to make. In the continuousness of his experience of Katherine, Rod sees what millions of viewers cannot due to the editing of the broadcast and he struggles internally between growing compassion and a swelling self-disgust that will compel him to take drastic action.

D.G. Compton is a writer whose fine prose focuses on characters, and he could have established him as a leading general novelist had he not committed himself to SF from the mid-sixties onwards, making his work an ideal read for those who enjoy the realistic settings of ➤➤ John Wyndham and ➤➤ J.G. Ballard. The moral dilemmas faced by individuals confronted by the implications of new technologies and changing times has been his perpetual interest, although he has tackled classic themes such as space colonization and aliens in some books.

**⬛ Film version:** *Deathwatch* (1974)

**⬛ Read on**
*Windows* (a sequel), *The Quality of Mercy*, *The Missionaries*, *Ascendancies*
Predicting reality TV: Nigel Kneale, *The Year of the Sex Olympics* (although this book is rare, a DVD of this teleplay is available)

# SAMUEL R. DELANY (b. 1942) USA

## NOVA (1968)

Lorq von Ray is a maverick and very wealthy space captain driven by an all-consuming obsession. It is the 31st century and the most precious substance in the known universe is the astonishingly rare element Illyrion, fuel for faster-than-light travel. Von Ray dreams of finding a new source of Illyrion, and thus altering the balance of power within the universe, but his quest demands that his ship plummet into the very heart of an imploding star. Gathering together a motley crew of adventurers and space drifters with little to lose, he prepares for the journey of a lifetime. Only his long-time enemies, former childhood friends Prince and Ruby Red, stand in the way of his close encounter with a nova.

In *Nova*, a book written when he was 25 years old and at his most exuberantly inventive, Delany took the tradition of the space opera and turned it on its head, giving what had always seemed a staid and conservative subgenre of SF the freedom to move into territory where no other writer had allowed it to stray. The result is a novel in which a thousand and one influences and ideas come together to create a rich vision of man roaming the star systems of the future. Echoes of sixties psychedelia share the page with reminders of the grail tradition in literature; tarot cards play a central role in revealing character and plot in the book. Delany's generous and optimistic portrait of a 31st century in which man and machine work in harmony (virtually everyone is a cyborg able to plug into any machine) and of the offbeat characters who people it (perhaps the most appealing is Mouse, gypsy maestro on a strange, multi-sensory instrument called the syrinx) shows why ❯❯ Algis Budrys once called him 'the best science fiction writer in the world'.

## 🥢 Read on

*The Jewels of Aptor*, *Dhalgren*
>> M. John Harrison, *Light*; M.K. Joseph, *The Hole in the Zero*; George R.R. Martin, *Dying of the Light*

---

### READONATHEME MINORITY REPORTS

Delany's kin: other black SF authors

Steven Barnes, *Lion's Blood*
Tobias S. Buckell, *Crystal Rain*
Octavia Butler, *Kindred*
Tananarive Due, *The Between*
Buchi Emechta, *The Rape of Shavi*
Nalo Hopkinson, *Brown Girl in the Ring*
Walter Mosley, *Blue Light*
John Ridley, *What Fire Cannot Burn*
Josephine Saxton, *Queen of the States*
Sheree R. Thomas (ed.), *Dark Matter*

---

# PHILIP K. DICK (1928–82) USA

## DO ANDROIDS DREAM OF ELECTRIC SHEEP? (1968)

In the not so distant future, the gap between the real and the artificial has shrunk. Androids almost indistinguishable from humans have been manufactured to work on Mars and other colonized planets of the solar system but some have escaped and arrived on Earth. Rick Deckard is a bounty hunter who has to track down androids masquerading as human and eliminate them. Six of the Nexus-6 models, the most advanced of all androids, are at large in the San Francisco area. Deckard must search them out one by one and 'retire' them. Use of the Voigt-Kampff Empathy Test is supposed to differentiate humans from androids but Deckard's experiences as he pursues the missing Nexus-6 models call into question both the value of the test and the essential difference between humans and androids. Not only does Deckard find himself emotionally and sexually drawn to Rachael Rosen, introduced to him as a member of the family that owns the Nexus-6 patent but actually someone who fails the empathy test, he begins to doubt the morality of what he is doing.

After Ridley Scott's film adaptation, released as *Bladerunner* in the year of Dick's death, *Do Androids Dream of Electric Sheep* became the author's best-known novel by far. In many ways, it is a paradigmatic expression of Dick's recurring motifs, ideas and obsessions. The shifting nature of reality, the difficulty of distinguishing between the natural and the artificial and the sneaking suspicion that paranoia may be the sanest response to experience are all present in its pages. Not only that but the world created for the book is filled with the quirky and unsettling products of Dick's unique imagination – the Penfield Mood Organ which users can set to induce particular emotional states, the strange religio-philosophical movement called Mercerism, the almost non-stop TV talk show hosted by the possibly android Buster Friendly and the electric sheep, substitutes for the increasingly rare real animals now prized as status symbols, which give this truly weird and wonderful novel its title.

🎬 **Film version:** *Bladerunner* (1982)

📖 **Read on**

PKD before Nexus 6: *Vulcan's Hammer*, *Martian Time-Slip*, *The Three Stigmata of Palmer Eldritch*, *Clans of the Alphane Moon*, *Dr Bloodmoney*

## READONATHEME: PKD TV

Philip K. Dick in the mass media

Alan E. Nourse, *The Blade Runner* (the SF novel from which the film of *Do Androids Dream of Electric Sheep?* drew its title)

>> William S. Burroughs, *Blade Runner: A Movie* (an unfilmed screen treatment of Nourse's novel)

>> K.W. Jeter, *Blade Runner 2: The Edge of Human* (the official sequel to the book and the film by Dick's friend)

Philip K. Dick, *Ubik: The Screenplay* (Dick's only screenplay, yet to be produced)

Philip K. Dick, *Confessions of a Crap Artist* (Dick's mainstream novel was filmed in France as *Barjo*)

Philip K. Dick, *A Scanner Darkly* (the third PKD novel to be adapted for the cinema)

Uwe Anton (ed.), *Welcome to Reality* (this anthology in honour of PKD includes his unfilmed teleplay treatment 'Warning: We Are Your Police')

Lawrence Sutin (ed.) *The Shifting Realities of Philip K. Dick* (contains two further TV outlines – a series plus an episode idea for *Mission: Impossible*)

## UBIK (1969)

In a world where telepaths and precogs – mutants who can predict the future – are for hire, Glen Runciter runs an agency staffed by individuals with even more bizarre psionic talents: inertials, who can negate the abilities of the psi-powered. When Runciter Associates lose track of the top telepath managed by their commercial adversaries, the Ray Hollis organization, Glen decides to consult his dead wife (whose consciousness is kept in stasis at a Swiss moratorium) for advice. Meanwhile Runciter's top agent Joe Chip also has a bad start to his day when his door refuses to let him leave his flat because he cannot pay the toll. Visiting a client on the moon, Glen and some of his team are assassinated in an explosion. Taking command of Runciter Associates, Chip prepares to take on Ray Hollis's psi cadre but begins finding cryptic messages from his dead boss appearing in uncannily mundane places and begins to suspect that reality may not be what it seems.

*Ubik* is one of Dick's most exciting forays into the world of human perception, dealing with one of his key themes: how can we know if what we experience is real? Combining Descartes with pulp motifs, asking serious philosophical questions while mocking traditional SF by breaking off into descriptions of the ridiculous clothing the characters of *Ubik* always seem to be wearing, this mindbending novel deliberately undermines our expectations of what SF is. Chapters are punctuated by ad-copy for an arcane, multi-purpose product called Ubik, whose possible use becomes clear as Chip and his colleagues slip back in time while the very universe itself seems to be degenerating. Dick later wrote a screenplay based on this fast-paced thriller, published only in a limited edition, which has sadly never been filmed, although features like *Scanners* and *Existenz* by director David Cronenberg reveal a clear PKD influence. *Ubik* is simultaneously accessible and challenging, a reality-twister whose exciting plot, harrowing ending and gleeful weirdness balance perfectly with a fundamental seriousness.

Dick died in 1982, having produced some fifty books. He was finally recognized outside the SF field after his death. He is now a major cult author and, in all probability, the genre writer of the twentieth century whose work will endure and be admitted to the canon of mainstream literature. *Ubik* is just one of many masterpieces PKD produced, a book that is representative of both his finest and most typical works.

## ⧉ Read on

Later PKD: *Galactic Pot-Healer, Our Friends from Frolix 8, Flow My Tears the Policeman Said, Radio Free Albemuth*; *VALIS*

# THOMAS M. DISCH (b. 1940) USA

## THE GENOCIDES (1965)

When unseen aliens decide to claim Earth for themselves, they sow the planet with seeds that grow into massive plants which begin to destroy the ecosystem. The plants adapt swiftly whenever new toxins are used against them and civilization itself begins to crumble. Then huge spherical incinerating machines descend to raze the cities, clearing the way for the extraterrestrial crop's full bloom. Following the struggles of a small American community as they try to survive the onslaught of the alien agriculturalists by burrowing into the roots of the monstrous vegetables, *The Genocides* is an invasion story with a difference: what chance can humanity have against beings who consider us to be nothing more than garden pests? Using ›› John W. Campbell's approach in pursuing an idea to its inescapable conclusion while refusing to conform to the psychologically dissatisfying conclusion invasion stories had suffered from since *The War of the Worlds*, Tom Disch had the audacity to defy decades of convention, consequently producing a marvellous debut that both broke new ground and upset traditionalist SF fans.

Overthrowing the old order was all part of the plan for ›› Michael Moorcock's *New Worlds* Magazine, attracting the rebellious young turks of the American SF scene such as Disch, ›› John Sladek and ›› Norman Spinrad, all of whom relocated to London to be involved in the front line of the New Wave revolution. *The Genocides* is packed with black wit, mordant observation of characters and the kind of self-consciousness present in the very best contemporary art. This was the start of a glittering career for Disch, whose novels, poetry and criticism have won him considerable acclaim even though he is regarded with suspicion by more conservative genre readers. Despite his occasional remoteness of tone, Disch is nevertheless a humane author whose highly accomplished and often very funny work marks him as one of the finest writers of literary SF ever to emerge from America.

### ⮑ Read on

*The Puppies of Terra* (aka *Mankind Under the Leash*), *Camp Concentration*, *Under Compulsion*
>> Samuel R. Delany, *Stars in My Pocket Like Grains of Sand*; >> John Sladek, *The Steam-Driven Boy*

# SIR ARTHUR CONAN DOYLE (1859–1930) UK

## THE LOST WORLD (1912)

The brilliant and belligerent professor of zoology, George Edward Challenger, has returned from a solitary trek through the Amazonian jungle with stories of a remote plateau on which prehistoric life still survives. A small expedition sets off for South America to search for the plateau. Accompanying Challenger are Professor Summerlee, a rival scientist with whom he squabbles incessantly, Lord John Roxton, a famous big game hunter, and Edward Malone, a young newspaperman whose reports back to civilization form Conan Doyle's narrative. Although the four men find the plateau, all but Challenger remain sceptical of the possibility that dinosaurs might have survived into the twentieth century. Their scepticism turns to wonderment when, out of the darkness one night, a great flying beast swoops down on their camp fire and carries off their food. It is a pterodactyl, assumed extinct for millions of years. Further surprises await the explorers. Herds of iguanodons roam the plain there; plesiosaurs and other marine reptiles swim in the lake. Most astonishingly, and most terrifyingly, a tribe of brutal ape-men lurks in the jungle. Captured by the ape-men, Challenger and his companions only survive through luck, intelligence and the firepower of their rifles.

The grand-daddy of all stories of men battling dinosaurs, from pulp fiction of the 1920s and 1930s to Michael Crichton's *Jurassic Park, The Lost World* remains a wonderfully thrilling narrative. Professor Challenger, quarrelsome, arrogant and childishly conceited, is almost as memorable a character as Doyle's most famous creation, Sherlock Holmes. The story is rooted in the assumptions and ideas of the Edwardian era in which it was written but its most dramatic moments – the first sighting of the pterodactyl, Malone's first encounter with the ape-men, the explorers' desperate battle for survival – can still capture the imagination of even the most jaded reader.

## ⮑ Read on

*The Poison Belt* (the best of several other Professor Challenger stories Doyle wrote)
>> Stephen Baxter, *Silverhair*; >> Greg Bear, *Dinosaur Summer*; >> Ray Bradbury, *Dinosaur Tales*; Michael Crichton, *Jurassic Park*; J.H. Rosny Aîné, *Quest For Fire*

# GREG EGAN (b. 1961) Australia

## PERMUTATION CITY (1994)

Some of the most startling and mind-bending ideas in contemporary philosophy derive from computer simulations and virtual reality. How can traditional beliefs in the nature of the self and human personality be sustained in a world where the boundaries between the 'real' and the computer-generated are less and less easily defined? This is the arena in which Greg Egan, an Australian computer scientist and SF novelist, has placed his most interesting fiction. *Permutation City* is an imaginative and engrossing exploration of the new worlds of subjective cosmology which virtual reality suggests may one day exist.

The year is 2050 and computing power has expanded to the point where it is possible for 'copies' of people to be downloaded into virtual environments. Sadly these copies are poor simulacra of flesh-and-blood beings. The power to mimic the real world exactly is still lacking and the copies live a sterile half-life in their virtual environment. Immortality is possible but it is an immortality of which the copies often weary, choosing to self-destruct rather than continue among its shadows. Paul Durham is a man who believes that he is able to offer copies a universe of their own – Permutation City – which is as rich and fulfilling as the real one and he approaches a group of wealthy men, who, since their bodies have passed away, exist only as copies, in order to fund his dreams of the future.

Egan, comfortable himself with the most advanced ideas in computing and with the speculations of transhumanist thinkers about the future, is a demanding writer who expects his readers to put in some work on his narratives themselves but he is a writer who can blend cutting-edge theory with intriguing storytelling to brilliant effect. *Permutation City* provides a rollercoaster ride through notions that stretch the mind in all directions.

### ⮂ Read on

Virtual (un)realities: Damien Broderick, *The Judas Mandala*; ➤➤ Philip K. Dick, *Lies, Inc.*, *A Maze of Death*; ➤➤ Christopher Priest, *A Dream of Wessex*; ➤➤ John Sladek, *The Muller-Fokker Effect*

# HARLAN ELLISON (b. 1934) USA

## THE BEAST THAT SHOUTED LOVE AT THE HEART OF THE WORLD (1969)

'A Boy and His Dog' is the definitive American New Wave story in this collection, winning the Nebula novella category and upsetting everyone: liberals, feminists, the right wing and Golden Age SF writers. It is 2024 in the former United States. Shortly after the millennium The Third War destroyed civilization and the only remaining cities are located deep underground, away from the radiation pits and the savagery of the surface, where vicious gangs known as Roverpaks reign supreme, foraging, bartering and killing to survive. Feral fifteen-year-old Vic is a 'Solo', eking out a ragged existence in this blighted, rubble-strewn post-apocalyptic landscape, alone apart from his sidekick Blood. The descendant of genetically enhanced lab animals, Blood is a dog – a telepathic canine with a better education than his would-be master. When Blood senses the presence of a girl (a rare commodity outside the downunder cities) and Vic decides it is time to claim this prize, the duo find themselves in situations they may be unable to fight their way out of. One of the few after-the-bomb tales to depict how raw and brutal existence after nuclear holocaust would really be while protesting and allegorizing the Vietnam War, 'A Boy and His Dog' inspired numerous 'survivalist' films and novels.

Harlan Ellison is one of the most decorated writers in the world: winner of over 100 awards, he works almost exclusively within short story and script forms, and consequently has remained little known outside SF circles and the USA. Editor of the landmark *Dangerous Visions* anthology, Ellison's TV work includes *Star Trek*, *Babylon 5* and *The Outer Limits* episodes (one inspired the film *The Terminator*), his uptight, intense prose, glinting with ›› Besterian colour, experimental verve and violent energy combined with a fierce polemical stance that ensured his explosive success in the sixties. This collection is the most representative of his SF (he also writes fantasy), containing twelve brilliant stories. Every word has been chosen with consummate skill, explaining why he is not only the most celebrated short story writer in the history of SF, but one of the greatest SF authors *per se*.

◀ **Film version:** *A Boy and His Dog* (1975)

≋ **Read on**
*Deathbird Stories*, *Approaching Oblivion*, *Strange Wine*
As an editor: *Dangerous Visions*, *Again Dangerous Visions*

# PHILIP JOSÉ FARMER (b. 1918) USA

## THE LOVERS (1969)

In the 31st century Earth is dominated by the fundamentalist Haijac Empire, a monotheistic religious state where women's figures are concealed by shapeless robes. Trapped in a loveless marriage, linguist Hal Yarrow has never shared sexual ecstasy with another being nor known the sheer joy of intellectual freedom. While most Earthlings seem content to await the second coming of their saviour who is supposedly exploring outer space until he returns on the Day of Timestop (from when eternal stasis shall reign), Yarrow is unfulfilled. Unexpectedly, Yarrow is selected for an expedition to Ozagen, a planet populated by simple yet sentient insects, the Laitha. Covertly, the Haijac Empire is interested in annexing the planet. Hal's excitement is short-lived when he finds himself chaperoned by the prurient, ultra-conservative Pornsen. During his examination of the languages of the Laitha, Yarrow encounters a woman claiming to be descended from a party of colonists stranded on Ozagen decades ago. Jeanette Rastignac is the most alluring female Yarrow has ever seen and their mutual attraction is obvious. Unable to resist Rastignac, Yarrow commits himself to a forbidden sexual relationship as it dawns on him that she may be human only in appearance...

A bold, versatile combination of religious, social and biological concepts, the original version of *The Lovers* appeared in 1952. Cited as being one of the first stories to introduce sex into SF, the tale shattered taboos and encouraged a new age of more mature genre speculation. His most exhilaratingly erotic work was commissioned by Essex House, a publisher specializing in pornographic SF: *The Image of the Beast*,

*Blown* and the magnificent *A Feast Unknown* all contain elements of fantasy and horror alongside floods of weird sex, metaphors for the latent impulses that underlie much SF and our subconscious reasons for reading it. Alive with high strangeness and ribald humour, Farmer is a playful writer whose love of pastiche and innovative flourishes never obscures his innate storytelling gifts. A master of the adventure story in the grand >> Burroughsian manner, he is equally at home with Planetary Romance as he is with 'biographies' of figures like Tarzan, whom he assures us actually exists. Although his most famous work is the *Riverworld* series, *The Lovers* is typically audacious Farmer, a perfect starting point for exploring the lively imagination and historic contribution of this generously spirited author.

## ⧤ Read on

More Haijac Empire PJF: *A Woman a Day* (aka *The Day of Timestop* or *Timestop*) and 'Rastignac the Devil' (from *The Cache*), the respective sequel and prequel to *The Lovers*

Other important PJF: *Doc Savage: His Apocalyptic Life* (a 'biography' of the pulp action hero and part of the author's massive *Wold Newton* sequence, influential over Steampunk SF), *To Your Scattered Bodies Go* (*Riverworld* Volume One), *Lord Tyger*

>> Philip K. Dick, *Cantata 140*; Michael Shea, *Polyphemus*; >> Jack Vance, *The Blue World*

# WILLIAM GIBSON (b. 1948) USA

## NEUROMANCER (1984)

It is the mid-21st century. Case is a former cyberspace cowboy, a hacker who interfaced his consciousness with the virtual realm of the net by connecting his nervous system to a PC, thieving data from corporations more powerful than nation states. Caught fencing information stolen from a vengeful client, Case is administered a psychedelic which burns away his matrix-manipulating expertise. Living on the edge in a lawless zone of dystopian Japan, his days seem numbered until he is kidnapped by Molly, a cybernetically enhanced assassin whose fingernails conceal scalpel-blade claws, her eyes hooded by mirrorshade lenses grafted on to her face. Molly works for Armitage, a mysterious figure who offers Case a chance to return to cyberspace and the reward of untold wealth. Case's neural odyssey will take him into a world of terrorist youth subcultures, software fences, enigmatic artificial intelligences and an orbital colony of Rastafarians. His story culminates in a deadly cyber-space run aboard a luxury tourist space-station, where he will risk brain-death in the ultimate virtual confrontation with Black Ice virus programmes designed to flatline the consciousness of any intruder.

Any summary of *Neuromancer* reads like a string of geeky IT clichés simply because it is the most influential work of SF in any medium in the last quarter of a century, its argot entering computing terminology. When first published *Neuromancer* was so cutting edge it defied the understanding of everyone except experienced SF readers and computing pioneers, but in the PC world of today its concepts and language are part of our everyday consciousness. The defining work of the cyberpunk genre, *Neuromancer* consolidated the position of SF as the most relevant literature of our times while securing a comfortable, effective meeting ground for the previously opposed schools of New Wave writing and hard SF. Glinting with the influence of high-concept prose stylists like ➤➤ Bester, ➤➤ Delany and ➤➤ Dick, *Neuromancer* additionally nodded at the hardboiled noir of American crime fiction and the inspiration of outsider rock music in its romantic identification with existentialist outsiders.

Since *Neuromancer* Gibson has produced seven further novels and attained the literary stature of ➤➤ Ballard or Don DeLillo in the process. *Neuromancer* remains unchallenged as the greatest single work of contemporary genre fiction and is perhaps the last true SF novel of genius.

### ⮔ Read on
*Count Zero, Mona Lisa Overdrive* (sequels to *Neuromancer*), *Burning Chrome*
Other seminal cyberpunk: ➤➤ Bruce Sterling (ed.), *Mirrorshades*; ➤➤ Bruce Sterling, *Schismatrix*

# JOE HALDEMAN (b. 1943) USA

## THE FOREVER WAR (1974)
Private William Mandella is a conscript. His lowly rank disguises his elite status, for like every soldier drafted into the army of the future, his IQ measures over 150. This special force is fighting a war waged in

interstellar space against an alien enemy – man's first contact with extraterrestrials during the colonization of distant planets has been a violent one. Earth is consequently at odds with an unknown species described only as Taurans. We follow Mandella's progress, from training on iceworld Charon, through mind-blowing stargate jumps that take his company many light years from Earth, to humanity's first direct engagement with the enemy. In what is merely months for Mandella, travelling on high velocity starships, years pass on Earth due to the effects of relativity and he returns home on R&R to find his homeworld radically changed. One of the few survivors of his unit, Mandella is promoted and shipped out to face the Taurans again, but this time he is fighting an antagonist whose technology has leapt ahead of ours, again due to Einstein's theories. If he endures, the next trip Earthside may be even more unsettling than his first.

Mandella is convincingly realized due to his similarity to the author himself: owner of a degree in physics and astronomy, Haldeman saw action in Vietnam, where he was wounded in combat and subsequently awarded the Purple Heart. The science of living and fighting in such a hostile environment as outer space is expertly described, while the disciplined use of relativistic physics in the plotting of the book – including dazzling starship chases – make for intoxicating reading. One of the best written hard SF titles ever, *The Forever War* is a key Vietnam document, praised by traditional genre readers and the most dedicated New Wave devotees alike. A distinctly anti-militaristic novel that succeeds in condemning rather than glorifying the follies of war, the book will be relished by anyone entranced by films such as *Full Metal Jacket* and *Starship Troopers*.

**≋ Read on**

*Forever Free* (sequel to *Forever War*), *Mindbridge*; *Study War No More* (collection of stories by various authors but edited by Haldeman) Lois McMaster Bujold, *The Warrior's Apprentice*; ›› Bob Shaw, *Who Goes Here?*

# PETER F. HAMILTON (b. 1960) UK

## THE REALITY DYSFUNCTION (1997)

By the 27th century mankind has established a domain that spans the stars. On Earth the Adamists (many of whom are members of old religious sects such as Christianity and Islam) live in domed cities that protect them from the rigours of a ruined environment. Meanwhile, the genetically engineered Edenists reside in artificial space habitats, their starpilots symbiotically linked in telepathic affinity with their biotechnological sentient starships. In a galaxy of thriving, vital diversity, *Homo Sapiens* reigns comfortably supreme. Young recidivist Quinn Dexter is one of a number of convicts routinely shipped to the newly colonized planet Lalonde, where he is destined to pay his debt to society by living in penal servitude to the growing population of this hot jungle world. Determined to escape back to Earth aided only by his hidden implants, his Satanist faith and a searing desire to avenge himself upon his betrayer, Dexter begins to wreak criminal havoc on Lalonde. He attracts the fascinated attention of an ancient alien hive intelligence that is surveying the planet, the being inadvertently opening a Pandora's box of unprecedented destructiveness when another living, malignant force engages with the universe and threatens to destroy reality itself.

Peter Hamilton is currently Britain's leading genre SF writer, enjoying massive bestseller status. *The Reality Dysfunction* was his break-through book, the first of the epic *Night's Dawn* trilogy (continued in *The Neutronium Alchemist* and *The Naked God*). Coming in at over a thousand pages packed with physics and biology, *The Reality Dysfunction* is not for the technophobic reader but it is aimed squarely at those who luxuriate in immense sagas whose main virtue is extra-ordinarily detailed societies. Although Hamilton reveals the influence of ➤➤ Bruce Sterling's shaper-mechanist stories (*Schismatrix*) and ➤➤ Iain M. Banks's epic sweep, this is classic space opera updated for the 21st century, suitable for an audience raised on post-*Star Wars* mass media SF. Whether Hamilton's position as a leading light of contemporary British radical hard SF will ensure his works achieve classic status is as yet unclear. To acquire an understanding of why the renaissance in UK fantastic fiction has proved so popular with a new generation of readers, *The Reality Dysfunction* is the only place to begin.

## ✒ Read on

*The Neutronium Alchemist, The Naked God, Pandora's Star, Judas Unchained*
Keith Brooke and Eric Brown, *Deep Future*; Ken MacLeod, *The Star Fraction*; Alistair Reynolds, *Revelation Space*; Adam Roberts, *Salt*; Charles Stross, *Singularity Sky*

# HARRY HARRISON (b. 1925) USA

## MAKE ROOM! MAKE ROOM! (1966)

Harrison may be best known for his Stainless Steel Rat books, a series built around the exploits of the reformed interstellar master criminal James Bolivar DiGriz but his finest achievement is probably this dystopian tale of an overpopulated New York. The year is 1999 and, as the millennium beckons, the city has descended into near chaos. It has 35 million inhabitants struggling to find food, shelter and the means of survival. One of them is the book's downbeat anti-hero Andy Rusch, a policeman who is drawn into the hunt for the killer of a racketeer and into a relationship with the dead racketeer's girlfriend. In the course of Harrison's deliberately unsensational story, Rusch finds little resolution to the problems of his personal and professional life. The killer is never brought to justice (and there is no sense that justice would really be served if he were); the girl leaves Rusch and his closest friend, Sol, an elderly room-mate with a line in homespun philosophy, dies. The policeman is left alone in melancholy contemplation of a city which, in its exponential growth, has left most human values behind.

The 1970s film version of *Make Room! Make Room!*, its title changed to *Soylent Green*, has its own cult status and its own devotees but does Harrison's novel a disservice. With its emphasis on the uncomfortable origins of the 'soylent' food used to stave off starvation in the city, the film moves into territory in which Harrison shows little interest. His book, so different from the light-hearted space romps for which he is famous, is an often bleak prediction of what the future might hold if human population continues to soar. The fact that the year in which Harrison's novel is set is now in the past rather than the future, and that it held few of the terrors he predicted, is irrelevant. *Make Room! Make Room!* still works as a powerful vision of a society crumbling under its own fertility and (who knows?) it might yet prove prescient.

**◀ Film version:** *Soylent Green* (1973)

**♻ Read on**
Lighter HH: *The Stainless Steel Rat, A Transatlantic Tunnel Hurrah!*
Overpopulation: ▸▸ Philip José Farmer, *Dayworld*; William F. Nolan and George Clayton Johnson, *Logan's Run*; ▸▸ Robert Silverberg, *The World Inside*

# M. JOHN HARRISON (b. 1945) UK

## THE CENTAURI DEVICE (1975)
By the 24th century, the Arab-Israeli conflict has spread throughout the galaxy as mankind has expanded its territory into space. John Truck is the louche, leather-jacketed owner of cargo ship *My Ella Speed*, known on numerous planets for boozing and drug abuse. Apprehended on Sad al Bari IV by an irascible female representative of the Israeli World Government and browbeaten by one of the repulsive religious fanatics known as Openers (who have replaced much of their skin with windows so that God can look within them), Truck flees the system to the immense spacedock that was once Great Britain. Attending the longest running party in the history of the universe, Truck continues to find

himself the quarry of myriad factions keen to press him into service and activate what they believe is the ultimate weapon. The Centauri Device is an artefact only explicable to its builders, a species of humanoids driven to extinction by Earthmen. As Truck's mother was one of the last surviving Centaurans, his DNA puts him in a precarious position of unwanted power where all the players are gambling for the highest stakes imaginable.

This ironic tale of Truck's picaresque attempts to avoid the inevitable is typical of M. John Harrison's rewardingly dense yet mercurial style. The author's past history as literary editor of (and major contributor to) *New Worlds* is abundantly apparent. Reminiscent of the high times when the new SF was a significant sector of underground publishing, the novel effortlessly employs such countercultural elements as antique Fender Stratocasters and interplanetary-scale dope dealing. Harrison's influence over contemporary radical hard SF is indisputable – he brought a multi-faceted complexity to space opera evident in the intricate works of ❯❯ Banks while echoing the feverishness of ❯❯ Bester. His finest works are his sublime short stories and the brilliantly observed mainstream novel *Climbers*, while his recent return to SF (*Light*) confirms him as one of Britain's most versatile and accomplished writers.

## ❧ Read on

Edward Bryant, *Cinnabar*; John Clute, *Appleseed*; Mark S. Geston, *Lords of the Starship*; Colin Greenland, *Take Back Plenty*; China Mieville, *Perdido Street Station*

# ROBERT A. HEINLEIN (1907–88) USA

## ORPHANS OF THE SKY (1941)

Should humanity need to travel to a distant system to colonize other planets, spacecraft designers face a severe difficulty unless a means of travelling faster than light is discovered: it would take so long to reach even nearby stars that the crew would die of old age before reaching their objective. If Einstein's barrier remains unbroken, one solution would be to build a Generation Starship, a craft so vast and self-sufficient that the crew spend their whole lives onboard, reproduce, die and so on until the voyage ends, when the descendants of the original astronauts set foot on a new world. The immense starship Vanguard is en route to Centaurus: everyone aboard knows this, but no one realizes what it means; even the elite fail to understand that there is anything outside the ship. In the aftermath of a mutiny generations ago, the original purpose of the mission has been forgotten and Vanguard has become a self-contained cosmos. Hugh Hoyland is selected for training as a Scientist. During a sojourn to the upper decks, he is captured by a gang of mutants who have made these outlying areas their home. Enslaved by the two-headed, philosophical Joe-Jim, Hugh begins to question the true nature of his world. Unless he can unite the mutants and the crew while overturning the dogma that has shaped his society, neither Hugh nor the Vanguard will fulfil their destiny. A cardinal example of conceptual breakthrough and therefore the epitome of SF itself, *Orphans of the Sky* is the seminal Generation Starship story, unsurpassed until ›› Aldiss produced the superb *Non-Stop* (1958). *Orphans* is typical of Heinlein's early work, forming part of his loose-linked *Future History* series, generally regarded as his most vital contribution to SF.

Although discovered by ➤➤ Campbell, Heinlein was older than the other *Astounding* authors. Easily the most assured, influential writer of the Golden Age of SF, combining logical extrapolation with adventurous verve, Heinlein's inspiration reached beyond the hard SF and right-wing speculative writers who are his spiritual offspring – without Joe-Jim (for example) we would probably never have had Zaphod Beeblebrox in Douglas Adams's parodic *The Hitch-Hiker's Guide to the Galaxy*. Regarded as a genius by writers as diverse as ➤➤ Ellison, ➤➤ Farmer, ➤➤ Dick and Stephen King, Heinlein is still considered the undisputed all-time grand master of genre SF.

## ⮑ Read on
Generation variations: ➤➤ Samuel R. Delany, *The Ballad of Beta 2*; ➤➤ Harlan Ellison and Edward Bryant, *Phoenix Without Ashes*; Garry Kilworth, *The Night of Kadar*; Alexei Panshin, *Rite of Passage*; Brian Stableford, *Promised Land*

## STARSHIP TROOPERS (1959)
Johnnie Rico is a trooper in a tough force of mobile infantry during a future war between the Terran Federation and the Arachnids, spider-like aliens from a planet called Klendathu. Through Rico's experiences, revealed mainly in flashback, Heinlein tells the story of the gruelling training inflicted on recruits to the mobile infantry (fewer than one in ten survive the rigours of the boot camp), the previous history of the Terran Federation and the development of its political structure, and the record of his hero's progress through the ranks from naïve recruit to battle-scarred veteran in charge of his own band of commandos.

Few SF novels have aroused such controversy over the decades as

Heinlein's militaristic epic. Although it won the Hugo Award in the year following its publication, *Starship Troopers* has been accused not merely of glorifying military values but of endorsing fascism. (The Terran Federation, which Heinlein clearly expects us to admire, is said by his most extreme detractors to be analogous to Nazi Germany.) If critics are not attacking Heinlein's politics, then they are badmouthing his literary skills. The writer and editor Anthony Boucher is not alone in arguing that the main difficulty with the book is that its author 'forgot to insert a story' and that it rapidly degenerates into a series of lectures about politics, history and philosophy thinly disguised as a novel. Despite (or perhaps because of) the controversy that has swirled around it since its first publication, *Starship Troopers* is an undeniably significant work in the history of the genre. It pioneered an entire subgenre of military space opera. In addition, many later writers, from ›› Joe Haldeman to ›› Orson Scott Card, owe a paradoxical debt to Heinlein in that they have written fiction in conscious opposition to the philosophy embodied in Johnnie Rico and his comrades. *Starship Troopers* is undoubtedly right-wing in its politics and unashamedly militaristic in outlook but it is also one of the finest coming-of-age stories in SF, a narrative that follows Johnnie Rico's rites of passage with the kind of detail and empathy that can be appreciated even by those readers to whom Heinlein's politics and philosophy remain anathema.

**⛊ Film version:** *Starship Troopers* (1997)

**⬙ Read on**
The later Heinlein: *The Door Into Summer*, *The Moon is a Harsh Mistress*, *I Will Fear No Evil*

Alternative soldiers: ➤➤ Harry Harrison, *Star Smashers of the Galaxy Rangers*; ➤➤ Norman Spinrad, *The Men in the Jungle*

# FRANK HERBERT (1920–86) USA

## DUNE (1965)

At the heart of Frank Herbert's massive and massively successful story of a future universe is a power struggle between three dynasties: the imperial family, House Corrino and two of its subordinate but still powerful clans, House Atreides and House Harkonnen. In Herbert's elaborately imagined galaxy, the most precious substance is the spice 'melange', crucial both to interstellar travel and the prolongation of life, and it is only to be found on the desert planet Arrakis. As part of a Machiavellian plot to destroy House Atreides, the Emperor places the family in charge of Arrakis. Travelling to the planet, Duke Leto Atreides and his son Paul are isolated from their power base and vulnerable to an attack from the Harkonnen. Leto is killed but Paul escapes into the desert where he joins forces with the Fremen, the blue-eyed warriors who inhabit its furthest reaches and ride the giant sandworms which are the planet's strangest and most powerful life-form. Accepted as a messianic figure by the Fremen, Paul Atreides moves to take his revenge on both the Harkonnen and the Emperor.

The world of *Dune*, with its battling dynasties, its weird witch-like female priestesses known as the Bene Gesserit, its bizarre fauna and its carefully structured religious mythology, brilliantly enhances traditional SF (the creation of alien societies and ecologies) with ideas and motifs taken from other fictional genres (historical novels of feuding medieval princes, sword and sorcery fantasy). When he created it, Herbert could have had little idea that he was beginning a franchise which was still to be selling books, films and computer games 20 years after his death. Herbert wrote five sequels to *Dune* and his son is co-author of new titles which continue to pour from the publishers. Unsurprisingly, none has anything like the power of the first book. The original *Dune* is a wonderfully eclectic novel in which Herbert gathers together elements from half a dozen fictional genres and uses them to create a narrative of great richness and depth.

 **Film versions:** *Dune* (1984); *Dune* (2000, TV series)

 **Read on**
*Dune Messiah, Children of Dune, God Emperor of Dune, Heretics of Dune, Chapterhouse Dune* (the five sequels written by Herbert)
Messiahs: **>>** Michael Moorcock, *Behold the Man*; Somtow Sucharitkul (aka S. P. Somtow), *Starship and Haiku*; **>>** Robert Silverberg, *To Open the Sky*

# ALDOUS HUXLEY (1894–1963) UK

## BRAVE NEW WORLD (1932)

It is the year of Our Ford 632 (or the 26th century in our own Gregorian calendar) and, in the world state run on the industrial principles first established by Henry Ford, the evils of war, poverty and unhappiness have apparently been abolished. Biological engineering creates a hierarchy of different citizens – Alphas, Betas, Gammas and so on – who are tailor-made for the tasks that society will demand of them. Psychotropic drugs and consequence-free sexual promiscuity provide the pleasures that keep all levels happy. Lenina Crowne, a conventional Beta Plus lab worker, and Bernard Marx, an Alpha Plus psychologist inexplicably dissatisfied with the apparently ideal life he leads, travel to the Malpais Savage reservation in New Mexico where an ancient mode of living still survives. There they meet John, son of an accidental refugee from the world state who ended up on the reservation. John returns with them to London where he confronts what he describes as the 'Brave New World' of apparent utopia (John is a reader of Shakespeare, unknown in the world state, and the phrase comes from *The Tempest*). Rapidly disillusioned with the world he discovers and convinced that the 'perfect' society is, in truth, a soulless hell, John retreats into isolation but he cannot escape either the notoriety his arrival has provoked nor his attraction to Lenina. Disaster and despair beckon.

Huxley, a polymathic novelist, essayist and social commentator, used his novel to explore the implications of a future society which has rid itself of most of what we would consider social evils. He realized that, in order to ensure one kind of human happiness and the eradication of many of the ills that plague contemporary society, so much of our humanity would be lost that the losses would outweigh the gains. His clear-sighted, unsentimental vision of a possible future is one of the great 20th-century dystopias and one that seems to have growing relevance in the 21st century.

### ⮑ Read on

Genetic engineering: Peter Dickinson, *The Green Gene*; Mick Farren, *The DNA Cowboys Trilogy*; Anne McCaffrey, *Dragonflight*; Geoff Ryman, *The Child Garden*; ›› H.G. Wells, *The Food of the Gods*

# K.W. JETER (b. 1950) USA

## DR ADDER (1984)

Hardboiled former boy soldier E. Allen Limmit manages the mutated staff of the company brothel at the Phoenix Egg Ranch, a battery hen factory populated by giant genetically engineered fowl whose intelligence matches their huge body size. Quitting this unedifying position, Limmit heads for LA bearing a briefcase containing a Flashglove, an outlawed CIA execution weapon he aims to sell to the infamous outlaw cosmetic surgeon Dr Adder. Sharp-faced, amoral and motorcycle-riding, Adder specializes in modifying the bodies of the aspiring hookers who haunt the Interface, LA's notorious vice and drugs district. The harrowing operations are bankrolled by rich punters with chilling sexual preferences for amputees and genital augmentation. The Interface is patrolled by the fanatical followers of Adder's nemesis,

Televangelist John Mox, whose Church of Moral Forces seeks to eradicate the degradation prevalent in the area by any means necessary, including extreme violence. Delighted with the Flashglove, Adder employs the bemused Limmit as his new surgical assistant. After a confrontation with the Moral Forces, Adder is forced to flee the Interface, electing to have a forearm removed and replaced with the Flashglove. Now activated, the device makes Adder even more lethal and unpredictable than his enemies ever thought possible.

*Dr Adder* is one of the strangest books in the history of SF and is strictly for adults only. Written in the early seventies, the book's intensity and tight contemporary style prefigures cyberpunk by ten years, while surpassing it in sheer attitude. No publisher would touch it until 1984, shocked by the uncompromising sexual elements, despite protestations from ›› Philip K. Dick that it was a work of genius. Alongside contemporaries ›› Tim Powers and James Blaylock, Jeter enjoyed the friendship of ›› Philip K. Dick and has furthered the tradition of surreal Californian SF the latter championed. Besides his other SF, Jeter has also worked extensively in horror fiction. *Dr Adder* is guaranteed to amaze even the most jaded SF fan and to reward any adventurous readers who tackle this radical and brilliant book.

## ☙ Read on

*The Glass Hammer*, *Death Arms* (sequels to *Dr Adder*), *Farewell Horizontal*, *In the Land of the Dead*
James Blaylock, *Land of Dreams*; ›› Tim Powers, *Dinner at Deviant's Palace*

# RAYMOND F. JONES (1915–94) USA

## THIS ISLAND EARTH (1952)

While going about his usual cutting-edge electronics research, Cal Meacham receives in the mail a highly advanced condensor that defies his knowledge of contemporary technology. Realizing that this strange piece of kit is not from his usual suppliers, Cal begins ordering other items from an unusual catalogue that came with the component. Following the cryptic instructions that arrive piecemeal with each gadget while relying partly on his own genius, he gradually builds a strange machine whose purpose is at first unclear to him. But when the device is fully assembled and activated, little does Cal realize that he is embarking upon an adventure that will take him far beyond his growing scientific knowledge and his insignificant home planet, for Cal has built an *Interocitor*....

Anyone familiar with the magic of the classic American SF films of the fifties will think they know the remainder of this story and will glow internally at the mention of the unfamiliar word above. But this novel, like so many that have inspired famous movies, diverges from the feature enough for those who cherish childhood memories to be newly engaged and entertained by the tale. For readers unfamiliar with the film, this thrilling story is a textbook example of the space operas that dominated the pulp magazines until the mid-fifties. Huge-craniumed aliens, flying saucers, intergalactic war and a plucky scientist hero, all are present here in their lurid yet carefully crafted glory. Embodying all the virtues that ❯❯ John W. Campbell saw in human beings, *This Island Earth* is tremendous escapism with a heart of gold and a pointed emphasis on rationality that great Golden Age SF required. One of the very best examples of this kind of writing, this engaging novel came right at the end of the Campbellian renaissance just as the sophistication of periodicals such as *Galaxy* and *The Magazine of Fantasy & Science Fiction* was about to usher in the stylistic innovations of the next phase of SF.

**◤ Film version:** *This Island Earth* (1955)

**⥸ Read on**
Fifties SF film adaptations: Jack Finney, *Invasion of the Body Snatchers* (aka *The Body Snatchers*); ›› Robert Heinlein, *Rocketship Galileo* (Film: *Destination Moon*); Mickey Spillane, *Kiss Me Deadly*; Philip Wylie and Edwin Balmer, *When Worlds Collide*

# LEIGH KENNEDY (b. 1951) USA

## THE JOURNAL OF NICHOLAS THE AMERICAN (1986)
Nicholas Dal is an American-born Russian émigré living quietly in Colorado. Known as Kolya to his remaining family, Nicholas is studying to be a librarian, a profession he hopes will keep him isolated from people. Kolya drinks copious amounts of vodka, but not in deference to a tradition from the old country or because he is an alcoholic. Kolya is a Telempath, cursed by an unwanted capacity to experience the

feelings of others – the clear spirit is his only defence against being overwhelmed by the emotions of those around him. Against his better judgement, Kolya forms a relationship with Jack, a young woman in his history class. Their sex lives are enhanced by Kolya's supernormal understanding of Jack's desires, needs and pleasures, inevitably leading to the couple falling in love. The Dals have always feared the scientific discovery of their despised gift, which is tainted by a rural tragedy in pre-revolutionary Russia. But Kolya's father is worried that a psychiatrist visiting the campus where his son studies is on the trail of the Dals and that it is only a matter of time before their true nature becomes public knowledge. When Kolya learns that Jack's mother is dying of cancer, he finds himself at grave risk of either psychic melt-down or an emotive revelation that could alter the way he feels about his hidden sense forever.

Comparing favourably with ›› Robert Silverberg's outstanding *Dying Inside*, Leigh Kennedy's first novel (shortlisted for a Nebula) is a tender yet powerful account of our willingness to shelter from involvement with others at the expense of the joy we can share with them. An ideal work to convert the general reader to the genre, *The Journal of Nicholas the American* is a splendid, character-driven novel that can only be claimed for SF by default, reminding us of the tradition of speculative fiction that has long been part of the mainstream. Kennedy's other works include a collection of engaging stories (*Faces*) and *Saint Hiroshima*. Her short fiction has continued to appear in magazines but she has been other-wise shamefully neglected, with two remarkable novels as yet unpublished.

## 🐚 Read on

SF for the mainstream reader: ›› Philip K. Dick, *Time Out of Joint*; Karen Joy Fowler, *Sarah Canary*; William Hjortsberg, *Odd Corners*; ›› Keith Roberts, *The Grain Kings*; Salman Rushdie, *Grimus*

---

### READONATHEME: ASSOCIATIONAL FICTION

Excellent general fiction by SF authors

›› Brian Aldiss, *Forgotten Life*
   A.A. Attanasio, *Wyvern*
›› J.G. Ballard, *Empire of the Sun*
›› Ray Bradbury, *Dandelion Wine*
›› Philip K. Dick, *In Milton Lumky Territory*
›› Thomas M. Disch and Charles Naylor, *Neighbouring Lives*
›› Harlan Ellison, *Children of the Streets*
   Mick Farren, *The Tale of Willy's Rats*
   Garry Kilworth, *Witchwater Country*
›› Michael Moorcock, *Mother London*
   James Sallis, *Death Will Have Your Eyes*
›› Robert Silverberg, *Gilgamesh the King*

---

# DANIEL KEYES (b. 1927) USA

## FLOWERS FOR ALGERNON (1966)

*Flowers For Algernon* takes the form of a series of entries from the journal of Charlie Gordon, the subject of an experiment in artificially increasing intelligence. In the beginning, Charlie is a gentle but intellectually retarded young man who works in a menial job. Chosen to participate in the experiment, Charlie slowly begins to develop. Eventually he reaches genius level and is as much at home with advanced calculus as he is with the more abstruse arguments of philosophy. Unfortunately, the experiment is deeply flawed. As the genius Charlie records, 'Artificially induced intelligence deteriorates at a rate of time directly proportional to the quantity of the increase.' In other words, Charlie is doomed to plunge back into the pit of mental incompetence from which the experimenters have briefly dragged him. His fate is foreshadowed in that of the laboratory mouse, Algernon, an earlier victim of the scientists' attempts to improve on nature, which regresses before his eyes.

Much of the brilliance of the book lies in the skill with which Keyes's prose style mirrors the different levels of intelligence possessed at different times by his central character. We follow Charlie in his own words as he moves from the stumbling, child-like language of his early diary entries through the dawning of his super-intelligence to the awful realization of his inevitable destiny. The novel had its roots in an acclaimed short story that Keyes wrote in the 1950s but the longer version takes the original idea and expands it into a gripping narrative of a mind gradually becoming aware of the disintegration that awaits it.

There have been many other depictions of enhanced human intelligence in SF over the decades, and it remains a potent theme in contemporary writing, but few have achieved the moving, relentless simplicity of Keyes's story.

◀ **Film versions:** *Charly* (1968), *Flowers For Algernon* (2002)

≋ **Read on**
(In)humanity: John Crowley, *Beasts*; ▸▸ Harlan Ellison, *No Doors, No Windows*; Charles Harness, *The Rose*; James Tiptree Jr (Alice Sheldon), *Her Smoke Rose Up Forever*; Bernard Wolfe, *Limbo 90*

# HENRY KUTTNER (1914–58) USA

FURY (1947)

It is the 27th century, six hundred years since Earth was vaporized by a nuclear chain reaction. Humanity survives in ornate undersea keeps beneath the oceans of Venus, unable to tame the brutal surface that teems with deadly life-forms. But the keeps have stagnated, evolving elaborate feudal structures ruled by the high-caste genetically modified Immortals, many of whom are nostalgic for the long-past local wars waged by the mercenary Free Companions. The spirit necessary to transcend the stifling decadence of the keeps exists only in two men: idealistic Robin Hale, seeking to conquer the unclaimed land to construct a spaceport and the ruthless Sam Reed, a squat, bellicose plebeian whose Immortal birthright has been cunningly concealed from him. On discovering how he has been misled by the elite, Reed responds with a blazing ire that neither Hale nor the remainder of Venusian society will escape.

In collaboration with his wife ›› C.L. Moore, Kuttner dominated *Astounding* throughout the forties, producing scores of sparkling short stories under a plethora of pseudonyms, both writers having enjoyed successful solo careers before their marriage. Since then scholars have spent thousands of hours researching their oeuvres in attempts to separate their joint efforts from their individual works. *Fury* has always been solely credited to Kuttner but it has long been known that the novel was a full collaboration. Although its tautness is characteristic of Kuttner, the often livid bloom of the prose marks Moore's sensual presence. Arguably an influence on ›› Bester's amoral *Übermenschen* of the fifties, *Fury* also exerted an influence over the New Wave when ›› William S. Burroughs lifted and dropped unedited, fully credited sections of *Fury* into the text of his novel *The Ticket That Exploded*. Burroughs' recurrent obsession with horrible physical addictions ministered by obscene alien creatures reflects *Fury*'s lethal fauna. Alone, Kuttner and Moore were both marvellous writers – together they were probably the finest team in the history of SF alongside ›› Pohl and Kornbluth.

## ⮒ Read on

*Clash By Night* (the exceptional prequel to *Fury*), *Mutant*, *Chessboard Planet*

Two of their most commonly used pseudonyms were Lewis Padgett and Lawrence O'Donnell, so watch out for collections under these bylines.

Planet Venus: C.S Lewis, *The Cosmic Trilogy*; Pamela Sargeant, *Venus of Dreams*

---

## READONATHEME TEAMWORK

Some great SF duets

>> Alfred Bester and >> Roger Zelazny, *Psychoshop*
>> Michael Bishop and >> Ian Watson, *Under Heaven's Bridge*
>> D.G. Compton and John Gribbin, *Ragnarok*
>> Philip K. Dick and >> Roger Zelazny, *Deus Irae*
>> Thomas M. Disch and >> John Sladek, *Black Alice*
>> Harlan Ellison et al, *Partners in Wonder*
   James Patrick Kelly and John Kessel, *Freedom Beach*
   George R.R. Martin and Lisa Tuttle, *Windhaven*
>> Larry Niven and Jerry Pournelle, *Oath of Fealty*
>> Frederik Pohl and >> Jack Williamson, *Land's End*

---

# URSULA K. LE GUIN (b. 1929) USA

## THE LEFT HAND OF DARKNESS (1969)

On the distant planet of Gethen, an envoy named Genly Ai has the task of persuading its rulers to join the interstellar federation known as the Ekumen. Like Genly, the inhabitants of Gethen are human. Unlike him, they are of indeterminate sex. Only during the period known as 'kemmer' do they become sexually active and each individual can be either male or female. Indeed, any one individual experiences periods of maleness and periods of femaleness throughout life. Accustomed to the strict gender demarcations of his own world, Genly finds the fluid sexuality of Gethen disconcerting, even disturbing, but he is most concerned with his diplomatic mission. His greatest ally appears to be a high-ranking politician in the kingdom of Karhide named Estraven, but Estraven is summarily despatched into exile by his king. Genly soon follows him out of Karhide and arrives in a rival political state. There he is imprisoned but eventually, after meeting Estraven once again, he escapes. Together the envoy and the exiled politician make an epic voyage back to Karhide, through the frozen and wintry landscape of Gethen. En route Genly and Estraven, who enters 'kemmer' during the journey, form a deep and loving relationship which is only ended, in tragic circumstances, when they approach their goal.

*The Left Hand of Darkness* is a remarkable novel for a number of reasons. In few SF narratives is an alien world conjured up so economically and poetically as Gethen is in Le Guin's book. Her lyrical descriptions of Genly and Estraven's winter journey across the planet are interwoven with the folk tales recorded by the envoy which subtly counterpoint his discoveries about Gethen and its people, and hint at an entire culture and civilization behind the events the reader witnesses. The issues of gender and sexuality which the narrative raises are unmistakably important but emerge easily and naturally from the story Le Guin is telling. There is no forced and strident preachifying in the pages of *The Left Hand of Darkness* but rather a sophisticated awareness of the difficulties both central characters face in their developing relationship. The novel is one of the most graceful, intelligent and thought-provoking examples of SF written from a feminist perspective.

## 🕮 Read on

*The Wind's Twelve Quarters*, *The Birthday of the World* (collections that include some other stories of Gethen), *The Telling*
Vonda MacIntyre, *The Exile Waiting*; Pat Murphy, *The Falling Woman*; Joan D. Vinge, *The Snow Queen*; Liz Williams, *Empire of Bones*

## THE DISPOSSESSED: AN AMIBIGUOUS UTOPIA
(1974)

Urras is a free-market planet, mildly authoritarian and wealthy, orbited by the barren moon Anarres. An austere but successful society which practises an almost religious anarchism has developed on the arid satellite, with individuals sharing goods as private property is virtually non-existent. The culture of Anarres was founded by Odo, a female political philosopher who fled with her followers from the laissez-faire of Urras. Brilliant theoretical physicist Shevek resides on Anarres, but he finds his ground-breaking work being suppressed by envious or doubtful colleagues. His genius recognized by physicists at the

Universities of Urras, Shevek is invited to lecture on the capitalist planet and to collect a significant academic award. On Urras Shevek finds himself a celebrity and begins to question not only his own beliefs but those of his hosts. Which world is the true utopia? Is Anarres only seeking to exploit his knowledge? As he debates these questions Shevek moves closer to confirming the secrets of the Principle of Simultaneity, whose technological applications will lead to the invention of the Ansible – a device that will allow instantaneous communication over vast interstellar distances.

A first-rate political meditation and a philosophical character study, *The Dispossessed* uses SF as the perfect arena to explore different theories of what would make an ideal society. Confirming her position as the greatest female SF writer to date, Le Guin's masterpiece is the finest utopian novel in modern literature. Offering no easy answers to the questions it poses, *The Dispossessed* is a thoughtful, rewarding book that examines the eternal question of the grass always seeming greener on the other side.

## ⮫ Read on

*Four Ways to Forgiveness*, *Orsinian Tales*, *Malafrena*
Charlotte Perkins Gilman, *Herland*; Robert Graves, *Seven Days in New Crete*; ›› Aldous Huxley, *Island*

# STANISLAW LEM (1921–2006) Poland

## SOLARIS (1961)

Kris Kelvin is a scientist specializing in the discipline of solaristics: the theoretical study of a distant planet whose ocean is a sentient organism. Since before Kris was born experts have explored and analysed Solaris, believing that they might one day make contact with the living sea enveloping this unique world that orbits a binary star grouping. But the trio of solaristicians currently resident in the hovering research station that perpetually drifts above the ever-mutating ocean have performed an illegal experiment in an attempt to communicate, bombarding it with x-rays. Kelvin is sent to investigate what is going on at the station and arrives to find the scientists unable or unwilling to talk to him about what has occurred on board since. Sensing their terror, Kelvin is soon alerted to the fact that there are impossible, uninvited guests walking the quiet corridors of the station. As he comes face to face with the eerie results of Solaris's efforts to acknowledge the cosmonauts, Kris delves deep into the immense archives of literature on the planet while attempting to come to terms with his feelings of guilt at his wife's suicide over a decade earlier.

Probably the most popular non-anglophone SF writer in the contemporary world, Stanislaw Lem was a Polish author who combined a fierce intellect, compassion and almost parodic affection for the clichés and strengths of genre SF (despite eloquent attacks on its failings) with a typically sophisticated European modernist approach: the simple yet vertiginous account of Kelvin's swift flight to Solaris and the poetic descriptions of the ocean itself reveal the extent of Lem's versatile genius. *Solaris* is an ornate and chilling book: its evocation of the haunted station, jammed with solaristic texts and unbalanced specialists hiding from their pasts make it one of the most resonant and lyrical 'first contact' stories ever published.

◀ **Film versions:** *Solaris* (1971, USSR), *Solaris* (2002)

≋ **Read on**
International literary SF: Kobo Abe (Japan) *Inter Ice-Age 4*; Karel Capek (Czechoslovakia), *The War with the Newts*; Dino Buzzatti (Italy), *The Tartar Steppe*; Herman Hesse (Germany), *The Glass Bead Game*; Ernst Jünger (Germany), *The Glass Bees*

# MAUREEN F. McHUGH (b. 1959) USA

## CHINA MOUNTAIN ZHANG (1992)

China Mountain Zhang is an ABC: American Born Chinese. In near future Manhattan, such status is of reasonable benefit to an academically under-achieving engineering worker of potential, for China's socialist revolution has swept America, dominating it. The great Eastern republic is now the leading country on Earth. After being manoeuvred into a blind date with his boss's daughter, Zhang loses his job and seeks his destiny. After spending time at an Arctic research station on Baffin Island Zhang eventually reaches China itself, where he studies to become an architectural engineer with an authentic touch of zen. While at university Zhang must disguise his outlawed sexuality while striving to become the success he has never realized he could be, tutoring settlers on Mars in electronics via the internet as his nascent talent flowers.

Maureen F. McHugh's first novel confidently describes an intricate, convincing future society that breaks some of the cardinal rules of SF: there are no stunning revelations that change the world of the story and the plot is not propelled by action or ideas. Instead, *China Mountain Zhang* is a slice-of-life character study, something common in the mainstream but resoundingly scarce within genre SF. Although Zhang is an ordinary person rather than a superman, an above-average talent whose distinguishing characteristic is that of homosexuality, the reader soon begins to identify with him as McHugh employs seductive literary skills in bringing him to life. Within a few pages one is rooting for Zhang, his stoicism and perseverance compensating for the lack of heroics. While employing a number of the conventions of cyberpunk (human-computer interfaces, microlite kiteflyers as sports heroes and so on), this is a sterling example of the thoughtful humanist philosophy female writers such as ›› Ursula K. Le Guin have brought to SF. The finest sinocentric future imagined by any writer in recent decades, McHugh's delicate yet sturdily constructed book, filled with filigree detail and unforgettable emotions, will be a revelation to dedicated SF fans and a surprise to general readers who mistakenly believe that science fiction cannot match the mainstream novel.

## ☞ Read on

Alternative sexualities: Gill Alderman, *The Archivist*; Storm Constantine, *The Enchantments of Flesh and Spirit*; ›› Samuel R. Delany, *Triton*
China ascendant: ›› Kim Stanley Robinson, *Years of Rice and Salt*; David Wingrove, *Chung Kuo*.

# BARRY N. MALZBERG (b. 1939) USA

## GUERNICA NIGHT (1974)

Author of over 100 books, Barry N. Malzberg shocked the world of SF when he won the >> John W. Campbell Memorial Prize for the third of his Cape Canaveral commentaries, *Beyond Apollo*. For instead of presenting an optimistic vision of mankind heroically conquering the solar system at the dawn of the space age that would have delighted the namesake of the prize, the author presented the bleakest picture yet of the kind of astronaut alienation that David Bowie's 'Space Oddity' and >> J.G. Ballard's command-module fatigue stories had already suggested. An undisputed master of creating narrators burning with cosmic angst and obsessed with grim, joyless sex, Malzberg surpassed himself with the intensity of *Guernica Night*. Sid is the young anti-hero in a future world of empty, luxurious pleasure and the use of instantaneous matter transmitters where The Church of the Epiphany rules over a society divided into encounter-groups. Despite the numerous ecstasies his world offers (such as role-playing in a recreation of the Kennedy assassination), the populace are fixated upon the newest kick, Final Tripping: good old-fashioned suicide. Drawn to self-destruction and eternally meditating on taking the Final Trip, Sid attempts to resist the overwhelming urge to plunge into the ultimate experience in a world gone mad.

A genius of the mordant, Barry Malzberg sensationally retired from writing SF in the late seventies, disgusted with the field, its self-imposed limitations, its core readership and the scant respect his writing had received from the mainstream. He has nevertheless published some SF since and he may one day be recognized as the greatest American genre writer since ▸▸ Philip K. Dick. His clever, severely dark work, full of unforgiving intelligence and black wit, will be greatly admired by admirers of ▸▸ Disch, ▸▸ Silverberg and the writers already mentioned above and devotees of general fiction ready for some of the most challenging, mature and rewarding writing in the history of the genre.

## 🕮 Read on

Malzberg on the pains of being an SF writer: *Galaxies, Herovit's World*
Spaced-out spacemen: *The Falling Astronauts, Revelations*; ▸▸ J.G. Ballard, *Memories of the Space Age*; Nigel Kneale, *The Quatermass Experiment*.

# RICHARD MATHESON (b. 1926) USA

## I AM LEGEND (1954)

Richard Neville is the sole survivor of a plague. He has burned the neighbouring houses to the ground and boarded up his windows. He forages and loots the city for sustenance and his means of survival, ensuring he is indoors by sunset. For Neville is not alone: the victims of the pestilence are around him still, neither alive nor dead, for they have turned into *vampires*... They come by night, braving Neville's barricades of garlic and crucifixes, striving to break into his fortress, while by daylight he tracks the fiends to their sleeping places and stakes their hearts. Raiding libraries, Neville begins a study of medicine. Eventually he discovers that the outbreak of vampirism is caused by a bacterial infection, a germ that is killed by sunlight. Is there time to find a cure?

*I Am Legend* is a sterling example of the kind of SF that is often popularly categorized as horror. This 'SF horror' is common in literature and film, using rationalist and scientific explanations for its explorations of fear, while the other types of horror use the supernatural or real life events as inspiration. Matheson is celebrated in the world of cinema as virtually all his novels have been filmed. *I Am Legend* has been filmed twice, neither version particularly satisfying. More importantly, the novel was arguably a source of inspiration for a whole subgenre of SF horror movies featuring flesh-eating zombies that began with George Romero's masterful *Night of the Living Dead*, which shares details of setting and the use of a scientific rationale with *I Am Legend*. Matheson's stark, gripping writing can be deeply moving: the greatest fear in his universe is that of utter loneliness. Matheson's concern for his characters – however doomed – illuminates everything he writes and he is always at pains to argue the tremendous importance of human dignity no matter how appalling his protagonists' situations.

◄ **Film versions:** *The Last Man on Earth* (1964), *The Omega Man* (1971)

⮷ **Read on**
*Hell House, Earthbound, What Dreams May Come*
Science fiction horror: William Hope Hodgson, *The House on the Borderland*; Stephen King, *The Stand*; Nigel Kneale, *Quatermass and the Pit*; H.P. Lovecraft, *The Call of Cthulhu*; ▸▸ John Shirley, *Crawlers*

# WALTER M. MILLER JR (1923–96) USA

## A CANTICLE FOR LEIBOWITZ (1959)

Walter Miller's output as a writer was small (two collections of short stories and one novel in his lifetime) but his influence has been substantial and that one novel is arguably the finest of all SF narratives set in a post-holocaust America. *A Canticle For Leibowitz* imagines a world many centuries after nuclear disaster has occurred in which scraps of pre-war knowledge are treasured and preserved by guardians who no longer understand what they signify. Divided into three parts, the book focuses on a Benedictine-style monastery, an island of culture in the sea of the new dark ages. The monks believe that their abbey was founded by the Blessed I. F. Leibowitz (actually one of the scientists whose work led to worldwide catastrophe) and so there is great excitement when, in the first part of the narrative, a young novice unearths ancient writings by Leibowitz. Some of the relics are merely grocery lists, unrecognized as such by the monks, but others are fragmentary blueprints of ancient machines. Six centuries pass and the Leibowitz memorabilia are providing hints of the technology that was destroyed. In the final part of the narrative, another six hundred years have gone. The old technology has been rediscovered and nuclear warfare is about to begin again. The abbot of the monastery despatches his monks and the Leibowitz relics into space to launch a new cycle of darkness and possible renaissance.

Cold War anxieties in the 1950s produced any number of novels which envisaged disaster and destruction in a nuclear war and speculated about the kind of societies that would later emerge but none did so with such intelligence and subtlety as *A Canticle For*

*Leibowitz*. Miller approached old questions of belief and religious faith from a new perspective. His memorable and ironic fable of the dangers of both ignorance and knowledge is as readable today as when it was first published.

### ও Read on
*The View From the Stars* (collection of Miller's 1950s short stories), *Saint Leibowitz and the Wild Horse Woman* (left unfinished at Miller's death, this novel was completed by Terry Bisson)
David Brin, *The Postman*; ›› Algis Budrys, *Some Will Not Die*; Emma Bull, *Bone Dance*; Pat Frank, *Alas Babylon*; Russell Hoban, *Riddley Walker*; ›› Keith Roberts, *Kiteworld*

# MICHAEL MOORCOCK (b. 1939) UK

## THE FINAL PROGRAMME (1965)
Jerry Cornelius is tall, slender, dark and in his mid-twenties. A sharp-dressed, sexually ambivalent figure, he is at various times a Jesuit, a physicist, an acid rock star, antisocialite and incestuous lover of his raven-tressed sister Catherine, a tendency that saw him ejected from the family home by his father, a mad scientist specializing in hallucinogenic devices. But old Cornelius has died and, sensing the imminent gravitational collapse of late sixties society as its contradictions and conflicts grow untenable, Jerry decides it is time to participate in a raid

on his former home by a cabal of dodgy businessmen and the rapacious IT maverick Miss Brunner. While his companions' target is a reel of microfilm containing the enigmas of his father's terminal project, Jerry's intentions lead to a confrontation with his narcotically challenged brother Frank and a tragic reunion with Catherine. A symbol of Swinging London, Jerry inhabits a quantum world where nothing is true and everything is permitted. An agent of chaos continually defecting between the forces of order and entropy, Jerry is a cool counter-cultural anti-hero, a needle gun in his palm, a flippant quip on his lips. Standing between **»** Bester's flawed, garish supermen and cyberpunk's studied hipsters, Jerry is the spirit of New Wave SF, his adventures first appearing in Moorcock's **New Worlds** magazine. Cornelius is also an avatar of the Eternal Champion, a figure who has numerous incarnations throughout the myriad parallel worlds of Moorcock's multiverse, the concept that links all the authors' fiction, from his classic heroic fantasies to his critically acclaimed social novels.

*The Final Programme* is the first of eight carnivalesque, anarchic books (and many short stories, some by other writers) to feature Jerry, his enemies and allies. It is a witty and exciting romp, whose progressively experimental sequels have non-linear structures that defy conventional approaches to plot. Those who enjoy exploring youth subculture will find that the dissenting Jerry Cornelius is as iconic as Hendrix, The Sex Pistols, **»** William Burroughs or whichever other Zeitgeist-defining personage is the flavour of the last fifteen minutes.

**⬛ Film version:** *The Final Programme* aka *The Last Days of Man on Earth* (1973)

## 🥢 Read on

*The Cornelius Quartet* (contains the immediate sequels to *The Final Programme: A Cure For Cancer, The English Assassin, The Condition of Muzak*), *The New Nature of the Catastrophe* (edited with Langdon Jones, Cornelius stories by various writers), *A Nomad of the Time Streams*

>> Brian Aldiss, *Barefoot in the Head*; Charles Platt, *The City Dwellers*

# C.L. MOORE (1911–87) USA

## BLACK GODS AND SCARLET DREAMS (collected 2002)

Northwest Smith: tall, startanned, scarred by blaster and talon, eyes like stainless steel, clad in frayed leather and spacer's boots. His stillness and cool demeanour belie a tendency for swift, decisive violence. A hard-drinking rogue and implacable adventurer, wanted on Terra but respected in every base dive of the solar system, a ray-gun at his hip, this is an Earthman unable and unwilling to keep out of trouble. Smith's life follows a pattern: another girl, another planet. On Mars he rescues the lovely, crimson-turbaned, coffee-hued Shambleau from a mob, only to discover that her feline eyes and incarnadine tresses offer a horrible yet voluptuous pleasure few men could resist. Another evening on Venus, Smith is lured into the forbidden house of the finest courtesans in the system by the stunning Vaudir, whose creamy flesh spills wantonly from her green velvet gown. Smith is tormented by black thirst for the immaculate beauties selectively bred by the Alendar, an extrasolar in humanoid form. Hunger jaded by peerless doxies, the Alendar finds Smith himself the most toothsome morsel on the menu...

*Scarlet Dreams* comprises ten of the very best pulp stories of the 1930s, originally published in *Weird Tales*. Smith is an archetypal figure, inspiration for every two-fisted existentialist in the history of space opera, from sophisticated spacefarers like ➤➤ M. John Harrison's John Truck to the cartoon heroics of Han Solo of *Star Wars*. In prose that is both brazenly lurid and carefully affected, Moore brought the one-dimensional icons of earlier space operas to vivid life with bold strokes of colourful, enticing eroticism that gives lie to the myth that there was no sex in SF before the fifties. This combination of simmering lust, vibrant fantasy imagery and flashes of horror set in a classic SF context ensures that Smith's stature as an icon of popular fiction will never fade. Catherine Moore, working both on her own and in collaboration with her husband ➤➤ Henry Kuttner, was the greatest of the early female SF writers and the current UK edition of her most famous works also contains *Black Gods*, the influential saga of Jirel of Joiry, probably the very first female protagonist in the heroic fantasy genre.

## ❧ Read on

*Judgement Night, Vintage Season*

Female magazine SF pioneers: Leigh Brackett, *The Long Tomorrow*; Judith Merril, *Shadow on the Hearth*; Zenna Henderson, *The People Collection*

# WARD MOORE (1903–78) USA

## BRING THE JUBILEE (1953)

Hodge Backmaker is born in the 1920s and grows up in a rural community in the Hudson River Valley, fascinated by the stories he hears of the War of Southron Independence seventy years earlier. In the war the Confederate South won its independence from the North and went on to become one of the world's superpowers. Hodge's dream is to become a great historian and scholar, studying the war, and he escapes his provincial backwater to head for New York. Even here, however, he finds himself in a world of decline and decadence. The city is not the vast, sophisticated metropolis we know but one of cobblestones, gas lamps and backwardness. Real power and cutting edge technology lie to the south in great cities like Leesburg. Hodge takes a job in a seedy bookshop but he still yearns for the life of a scholar and applies to join an eccentric academic community called Haggershaven. He is accepted and, in Haggershaven's ivory towers, he finds some kind of happiness. One of his fellow scholars is Barbara Haggerswell, descendant of the community's founder and a brilliant physicist who is working on a time machine. When Barbara's experiments prove successful, Hodge decides to fulfil every historian's dream of witnessing at first hand events of which he has so far only read. He uses the time machine to travel back into the past and arrives at Gettysburg on the eve of the great battle where his presence is about to divert history on to another path.

First published in 1953, *Bring the Jubilee* is one of the great works of alternative history. Unlike so many examples of this subgenre, in which most of the energy goes into the invention of the parallel world and little into plot or characterization, Moore's book not only creates a convincing alternative America but it tells a gripping story about a likeable and interesting individual.

### ⮂ Read on

*Greener Than You Think* (Moore's first SF novel is a satirical catastrophe novel in which a mutated form of grass gradually spreads until it covers the entire world)

›› Gregory Benford (ed.), *Hitler Wins*; ›› Philip K. Dick, *The Man in the High Castle*; ›› Christopher Priest, *The Separation*; ›› Robert Silverberg, *Roma Eterna*; Harry Turtledove, *The Guns of the South*

# RICHARD MORGAN (b. 1965) UK

## ALTERED CARBON (2002)

A former member of an elite military corps, neurochemically treated criminal Takeshi Kovacs operates on Harlan's World, hundreds of light years from Earth, a planet he has never visited. Killed by commandos in the aftermath of a sting, Kovacs's consciousness is digitally frozen, the equivalent of prison in the twenty-sixth century. Only the poor die now: the majority of people have their personality backed up regularly and recorded in microstacks embedded in the flesh at the back of the neck, ready to be retrieved and 'resleeved' in a new body that previously belonged to someone else, the original owner in penal storage or actually dead.

Kovacs's mind is beamed across space at high speed to Earth via a needlecast transmission and downloaded into a new sleeve. One of the mega-rich near immortals known as 'Meths' is willing to offer Kovacs a deal for some detective work – the supersoldier must find out who murdered his now resurrected client and why, the prize being early release from a century of penal stasis and a handsome fee. Ripping along at a high-adrenalin pace for all of its 500-plus pages, *Altered Carbon* is a skydive rush of a novel that combines the hyperreal glitter of the best cyberpunk with the compulsive quality of bestseller-list thrillers. Much has been made of the book's debt to *noir* fiction, but a contemporary hard-boiled writer like James Crumley would be a more fitting comparison than the more chivalric Raymond Chandler, given Morgan's penchant for extreme violence, explicit sex and Gordian-knot plotting.

A supreme example of how authentic cyberpunk can enliven (and be enlivened by) an angle that would not be out of place in a Hollywood blockbuster, *Altered Carbon* is a refreshing British alternative to the worthy yet sometimes dull 'sense of wonder' hard SF that otherwise dominates the contemporary genre scene. Anyone who enjoyed *Neuromancer* and the films *The Bourne Identity* and *The Matrix* needs to catch up with Richard Morgan.

## 🐦 Read on

*Broken Angels, Market Forces*
Neal Asher, *Gridlinked*; Steve Aylett, *Shamanspace*; Paul McAuley, *Fairyland*

## READONATHEME THIS IS THE POSTMODERN WORLD

Elizabeth Bear, *Hammered*
Bruce Bethke, *Headcrash*
>> Pat Cadigan, *Patterns*
Marianne De Pierres, *Nylon Angel*
>> K.W. Jeter, *Noir*
Tom Maddox, *Halo*
>> Michael Moorcock, *Firing the Cathedral*
>> Bruce Sterling, *Zeitgeist*
Walter John Williams, *Hardwired*
Jack Womack, *Random Acts of Senseless Violence*

# LARRY NIVEN (b. 1938) USA

## RINGWORLD (1970)

In the 29th century, the world has become a boring succession of parties and empty pleasures for Louis Wu, a 200-year-old space adventurer still at the peak of his physical fitness. When he is offered the chance to explore the Ringworld, a gigantic artificial structure many millions of times the size of Earth, he seizes it. Together with three companions – a woman named Teela Brown, who has been genetically selected to be a lucky individual; Nessus, a member of an advanced alien species known as Pierson's Puppeteers; and the ferocious Speaker-to-Animals, one of the cat-like aliens, the Kzinti – he departs for Ringworld. Their ship crash-lands on the megastructure and the foursome must find a way of getting back into space. They begin an exploration of Ringworld and the strange ecosystems and civilizations that have evolved on it.

Niven's novel is a relatively short one but there is much in it to hold the reader's attention. The descriptions of what the explorers encounter are compelling and imaginative; the tensions between the very different individuals forced into co-operation and competition provide an ever-present undercurrent in the narrative. None the less, the real star of the novel is the Ringworld itself. The vast engineered 'planet', both skilfully conceived and rigorously defined in terms of potential future physics and technology, is a triumph of the imagination and dominates the novel to which it gives its name, overshadowing the human and alien characters let loose on its surface. Niven went on to write several sequels to the original book, in which he explored the further possibilities of his creation, and he has also produced a number of large-scale sagas of alien invasion and planetary colonization in collaboration with Jerry Pournelle. Unlike many SF writers of his generation, who tend towards the dystopian, Niven remains basically an optimist and his celebrations of the transforming power of engineering and technology are among the most exciting and rewarding examples of hard SF in the last forty years.

## 📚 Read on

*The Ringworld Engineers*, *The Ringworld Throne*, *Ringworld's Children* (the three sequels to the original novel), *World of Ptavvs*
Alien artefacts: ▶▶ Greg Bear, *Eon*; ▶▶ Arthur C. Clarke, *Rendezvous With*

*Rama*; **>>** Bob Shaw, *Orbitsville*; John Varley, *Titan*; Colin Wilson, *The Space Vampires*

# GEORGE ORWELL (1903–50) UK

## NINETEEN EIGHTY-FOUR (1949)

In the mid-fifties massive political revolutions grip the world while atom bombs drop all over the West and Russia. During the early sixties, Britain, Australasia and South Africa merge with the USA to form the super-state Oceania, while the USSR absorbs Europe to create Eurasia. In the orient, Eastasia forms. Africa and the Middle East are the theatre in which the three super-states wage their wars. Oceania is sometimes in alliance with one super-state and at odds with the other, but the coalitions shift constantly, friends becoming enemies and vice versa. These megapowers are harsh, inhuman police states, grey post-holocaust wastelands where voluntary mind control, propaganda, purges, torture and even language itself are used to rewrite history, their structures maintained by occupying their citizens with military manufacturing and ritualized hatred of their enemies. Winston Smith lives in London, capital of Airstrip One. Working at The Ministry of Truth, Smith falsifies the newspaper articles of the past to reflect the current wisdom of The Party, which is shaped by an ideology called Ingsoc and led by the messianic Big Brother. Party members are surrounded almost everywhere by the Telescreens, which both broadcast and receive: while being continually barraged by propaganda, the populace can be surveyed at any time by the leather-clad Thought Police. Smith (who secretly hates The Party and the austere society of Oceania) revolts by keeping a diary, starting a love affair with a younger woman and forming a strange bond with O'Brien, a member of the bureaucratic Inner Party, whom he believes is a member of a secret rebel organization called The Brotherhood. Smith's defiance condemns him to The Ministry of Love and the unbearable reality of Room 101...

George Orwell was the finest political novelist ever and his most famous work is one of the best-known books in history, acclaimed as a classic almost immediately after publication. A supreme satire of totalitarian leaders and a searing condemnation of their oppressive philosophies that shaped Europe after the First World War, its devices are also mirrored in our contemporary life – CCTV, WMD, power-mad fear-mongering dictators and the debasement of English through text messaging. Overwhelmingly depicting a nightmare society with relentless, grim realism and unfailingly clever invention, *Nineteen Eighty-Four* is the greatest of all dystopian novels. Although some readers do not automatically regard the book as science fiction, Orwell's creation of Newspeak, Floating Fortresses, novel-writing machines and his predictions of the Cold War, Mutually Assured Destruction, brainwashing, a lottery-obsessed proletariat, Third World carnage and helicopters in guerrilla warfare mark him as an SF visionary of world-building genius whose prophetic, persuasive ideas have become part of our everyday language.

📽 **Film/TV versions:** *Nineteen Eighty-Four* (BBC TV, 1954); *1984* (1955); *Nineteen Eighty-Four* (1984)

## ☜ Read on

Orwell's thematic precursors to *Nineteen Eighty-Four*: *Coming Up For Air*, *Animal Farm*

Orwell's dystopian precursors: Yevgeny Zamyatin, *We* (USSR); Jack London, *The Iron Heel*; ➤➤ Keith Roberts, *Molly Zero*

# FREDERIK POHL (b. 1919) USA

## MAN PLUS (1976)

Experts advise the President that problems plaguing poorer countries and the expansionist policies of the Chinese mean that global war and extinction are inevitable. Buoyed by America's burgeoning military-industrial combine, the President gives the green light for project Man Plus: the creation of a pantropic cyborg – a surgically engineered man who can live on Mars and prepare the planet for colonization. Roger Torroway is a typical astronaut: atheletic, clean-cut, married, antiseptically bland, conventionally glib. Catapulated to fame by his presence on board a space station that participates in the rescue of a stricken Russian Mercury mission, Torroway has 'the right stuff'. Working as an observer on the project when the astronaut selected for the bionic augmentations dies from the traumas his body has undergone, Torroway finds himself substituted in the role of Man Plus. We follow the conversion of man to machine in unflinching, persuasive detail. Torroway adapts to the replacement of his eyes and the grafting of solar-panel wings but some unexpected operations come as a shock to the astronaut and reader. Uncompromisingly depicting with surgical coolness the mental anguish Torroway experiences as he is transformed into something both more and less than human, *Man Plus* anticipates cyberpunk and withholds nothing in its examination of the merciless advance of scientific logic as political expediency casts ethics by the wayside. Narrated in a dispassionate voice by an anonymous narrator whose identity is key to the story, the chilling flatness of *Man Plus* erupts when Torroway sets foot on Mars itself.

Pohl began his career as a magazine editor in 1940. He wrote extensively with ›› Jack Williamson and C.M. Kornbluth, with whom he produced the classic *The Space Merchants* (1953), which describes a future world dominated by advertizing. This novel had a huge impact in determining the possibilities for 1950s' social SF: although his work began in the ›› Campbellian era, Pohl has always helped to determine the future of the genre through measured work as an editor, anthologist and writer. With George W. Bush urging NASA toward Mars while questions of American hegemony remain contentious, *Man Plus* is surprisingly relevant.

## ⧉ Read on

*Gateway, Jem*, (with C.M. Kornbluth) *Wolfbane*
›› James Blish, *The Seedling Stars*; David R. Bunch, *Moderan*; Martin Caidin, *Cyborg*; Vonda MacIntyre, *Superluminal*; ›› Jack Williamson, *Terraforming Earth*

# TIM POWERS (b. 1952) USA

## THE ANUBIS GATES (1983)

Brendan Doyle is a Californian devotee of William Ashbless, an obscure poet and contemporary of Coleridge whose life and career have been virtually ignored by academics. Receiving an offer of $20,000 to travel to London to act as a consultant on a project run by DIRE, a leading scientific research organization, Doyle is intrigued. But his curiosity is replaced by incredulity when DIRE's resident genius, J. Cochran Darrow, says that he wishes to send Doyle back in time to 1810 to witness one of Coleridge's lectures. Darrow has discovered that time is like a frozen river whose icy surface is punctuated by occasional holes and, using his technological prowess, he conveys Doyle back to early 19th-century London. What begins as a unique opportunity for Doyle becomes a nightmare when he discovers himself unable to return to 1983, finding the dank midnight streets of the metropolis stalked by a myriad of carnivalesque monstrosities. As he descends further into the pandemonium of the capital, Doyle is ensnared in the machinations of several outlandish characters both human and otherwise. Eventually, a shattering personal transformation allows him to learn more about the mysterious Ashbless than he ever wanted to know.

*The Anubis Gates* is a superior classic of the steampunk canon: a nostalgic yet often postmodern subgenre of SF that celebrates the London(s) of Dickens, ›› Wells, Robert Louis Stevenson and G.K. Chesterton. Steampunk characteristically depicts the fog-shrouded, Hyde-haunted city as being rife with secret societies, nefarious conspiracies, ultra-advanced industrial revolution technology and supernatural beings. Popularized by comics like *The League of Extraordinary Gentlemen*, steampunk was also practised by Powers' friends James Blaylock and ❯❯ K.W. Jeter. A sumptuous tapestry of literary scholarship, fierce horror and admirable inventiveness, *The Anubis Gates* is a fine entrée into the catalogue of a writer whom cinema-conscious readers should be giving their attention.

## ❧ Read on

*The Drawing of the Dark, On Stranger Tides*
Steampunk: James P. Blaylock, *The Digging Leviathan*; Mark Gatiss, *The Vesuvius Club*; ❯❯ William Gibson and ❯❯ Bruce Sterling, *The Difference Engine*; ❯❯ K.W. Jeter, *Infernal Devices*; ❯❯ Christopher Priest, *The Space Machine*

## READONATHEME GETTING THE FEAR

Outstanding ghost and horror fiction by genre authors

Clive Barker, *The Hellbound Heart*
Robert Bloch, *Psycho*
❯❯ Ray Bradbury, *Something Wicked This Way Comes*
James Lee Burke, *In the Electric Mist With Confederate Dead*
Richard Cowper, *Shades of Darkness*
Stephen Gregory, *The Cormorant*
William Hjortsberg, *Falling Angel*
Shirley Jackson, *The Haunting of Hill House*

Fritz Leiber, *Conjure Wife*
George R.R. Martin, *Fevre Dream*
Dan Simmons, *The Song of Kali*
Lisa Tuttle, *Gabriel*

# CHRISTOPHER PRIEST (b. 1943) UK

## THE GLAMOUR (1984)

Television cameraman Richard Grey is convalescing at a nursing home in Devon, recuperating from injuries sustained in a terrorist bombing. Grey suffers from amnesia: he cannot recall the weeks prior to the explosion. An insipid young woman called Susan Kewley visits him and insists she was his girlfriend, although Grey has no memory of her. Despite her nebulous quality, Grey encourages the association as a means of unlocking the vacant chapter in his past. Soon he realizes that there was a third person interfering with their relationship, a vague yet somehow ever-present young man whose very existence threatens Grey's hold on reality... To describe *The Glamour* any further would ruin the story: suffice to say that it is a spellbinding and original narrative which is also a homage to one of the famous works of H.G. Wells. Opening the book awakens an obsessive hunger in the reader that leaves them unable to lay it aside until its enigmas are fully experienced.

Christopher Priest is claimed to have coined the term 'New Wave' to describe the British experimental literary SF of the sixties. Never strongly associated with **New Worlds**, Priest is close to >> Wyndham in his desire to ensure that SF is recognized as being part of a British literary tradition that existed in the mainstream before the Americanization of the genre via the pulps. After the incisive, stark pure SF that comprises his early oeuvre, addressing politics, the nuclear threat and problems of perception (notably in his uniquely brilliant **Inverted World**, which employs a dazzling geometrical concept), Priest has consistently tackled how we experience reality subjectively, warping the fabric of our senses with an intensity >> Philip K. Dick would have applauded. Priest's painstaking, detached prose convinces us utterly with the credibility of his characters and settings while demanding we question our most fundamental assumptions about reality and fiction. In 1983 **Granta** magazine selected him as one of Britain's best young novelists (alongside Amis, Barnes, Ishiguro and Rushdie among others) and the recent film of his novel **The Prestige** will have introduced his books to a wider audience. One of the finest writers of literary SF ever, Priest's achievements stand alongside those of >> Ballard as the epitome of indefinable writing: there is no consensus on whether **The Glamour** is SF or not and there can be no better reason to read Priest than this uncertainty.

## 🕮 Read on

*Indoctrinaire, Fugue For a Darkening Island, The Affirmation, The Extremes*
>> J.G. Ballard, *Running Wild*; >> M. John Harrison, *The Course of the Heart*; >> Keith Roberts, *Grainne*

## READ ON A THEME ENGLAND, MY ENGLAND

Particularly British speculations

Joan Aiken, *The Wolves of Willoughby Chase*
Eric Brown, *A Writer's Life*
>> John Brunner, *The Shift Key*
>> D.G. Compton, *Scudder's Game*
Michael Coney, *Hello Summer, Goodbye*
Richard Cowper, *The Twilight of Briareus*
Richard Jefferies, *After London: Wild England*
Vincent King, *Candy Man*
Dick Morland (Reginald Hill), *Albion! Albion!*
>> Keith Roberts, *Kaeti & Company*
Emma Tennant, *The Crack*
>> John Wyndham, *The Seeds of Time*

# KEITH ROBERTS (1935–2000) UK

## PAVANE (1968)

Keith Roberts was one of the most offbeat and exciting talents that British SF has ever produced. The cautiousness of publishers and his own difficult, cantankerous personality combined to create circumstances in which his work often failed to gain the audience it deserved but all his books have an originality that few other writers can match. Nearly forty years after it was written, *Pavane* remains one of the greatest of all works of alternative history, perhaps only matched in its intensity by ›› Philip K. Dick's vision of an America that might have been in *The Man in the High Castle*.

In the world that Roberts so skilfully creates, the Protestant Reformation did not take place, the Spanish Armada sailed to victory and Elizabeth I was assassinated. The book, a sequence of linked stories, is set in the 1960s and the Catholic Church still reigns supreme in Britain, its institutional face firmly set against the advance of science and technology. Yet the forces of material progress cannot be entirely stifled and the possibilities of change lurk at the peripheries of the stories that Roberts chooses to tell. *Pavane* takes its title from the name of a stately court dance of the 16th century and its 'measures', the individual stories, conclude with a 'coda' in which the contrasts between our own reality and the alternative that Roberts has imagined are made more explicit. With its tales of monks lovingly maintaining centuries-old traditions, of would-be inventors dreaming of change and of semaphore operators (the long-distance communicators of the age) exiled in remote signalling stations, *Pavane* is a peculiarly English vision of an alternative past. Roberts's own love for the rural landscapes of the West Country, for the folklore of fairies and hobgoblins, and for the ruined remains of castles and churches emerge in a linked narrative that blends together potential versions of past and present into a mesmerizing whole.

## ⮷ Read on
*The Furies, Machines and Men, Ladies From Hell*

Post-Armada alternatives: Kingsley Amis, *The Alteration*; ›› John Brunner, *Times Without Number*

# KIM STANLEY ROBINSON (b. 1952) USA

## RED MARS (1993)

Mars has long intrigued writers of speculative fiction but many of the novels set on the red planet, from ›› Edgar Rice Burroughs's extravagant fantasies to ›› Philip K. Dick's characteristically offbeat visions of a desert Mars, have paid little attention to the genuine science that might lie behind any future manned missions there. Kim Stanley Robinson's trilogy, of which *Red Mars* is the first, is the finest attempt in contemporary SF to imagine how the colonization of the planet could progress. Beginning with the arrival in the 2020s of the pioneering colonists, the First Hundred, the narrative follows the gradual progress of the Martian settlement as it grows from tiny outpost of Earth to self-contained world. The readers see the shifting alliances and antagonisms between the first settlers, the growth of a political and scientific debate between those who wish to move ahead with terraforming the planet and those who advocate a more cautious approach to meddling with Mars's natural environment, and the tensions that arise when further settlers arrive to join the First Hundred.

Robinson's imagination is clearly stirred by the potential of manned travel to Mars. His descriptions of the Martian landscape and the changes effected by man's intervention are breathtaking in their lyricism and attention to detail. He wants his book to be as scientifically accurate as it can be but there is much more to *Red Mars* than just scientific speculation. His characters are rounded and believable people, caught up in extraordinary, pioneering circumstances, whose political alliances, arguments and interrelationships are brought vividly to life. Hard science, weird geology and convincing psychology combine in what is a remarkable, epic account of the formation of a new world and a new society. This, the reader comes to believe, is what the future colonization of Mars could well be like.

## 🐾 Read on

*Green Mars*, *Blue Mars* (the two other volumes in the Martian trilogy)
Ben Bova, *Titan*; David Brin, *Sundiver*; ▶▶ Robert A. Heinlein, *The Man Who Sold the Moon*; Cecilia Holland, *Floating Worlds*; ▶▶ Larry Niven and Jerry Pournelle, *Lucifer's Hammer*

# JOANNA RUSS (b. 1937) USA

## THE FEMALE MAN (1975)

Four women experience life in very different ways in four parallel worlds. In a world not radically dissimilar to contemporary America, Joanna suffers from male oppression and condescension. Jeannine lives in a reality that seems like a paradigm of male fantasies about earlier days when women knew their place and the relationships between the sexes were uncomplicated by female demands for equality. The Second World

War has not taken place and the country is still suffering from the effects of the Great Depression. On the planet Whileaway Janet lives in a women-only society where men are absent and unmissed. The fourth character is Jael, aka Alice Reasoner, a cyborg man-killer from a dystopian future in which men and women, living separately in Manland and Womanland, engage in constant warfare. As boundaries between these parallel worlds break down, Russ charts the interactions between the women, each possessing a personality shaped by the society in which she lives.

Feminist writers produced some of the most inventive and challenging SF of the 1970s, as women staked their claims in a genre that had long been dominated by men. Joanna Russ proved one of the most outspoken and uncompromising women writers who emerged in the late 1960s and early 1970s and *The Female Man*, a book that can prove uncomfortable reading for any man, is a novel that boldly challenges all preconceptions about gender and the 'natural' relation-ship between the sexes. Using SF to undermine conventional thinking and to imagine alternatives, Joanna Russ creates an angry, bitterly comic work of fiction that turns a series of reflecting mirrors on oppressive and patriarchal societies. Through the experiences of her four everywomen she charts both the injustice of the present day and the potential paths towards liberation, and she does so in compelling narratives that demand the attention of her readers.

## 🕮 Read on

*The Adventures of Alyx, We Who Are About To...*
Margaret Atwood, *The Handmaid's Tale*; Suzy McKee Charnas, *Walk to the End of the World*; Gwyneth Jones, *Divine Endurance*; Marge Piercy, *Woman on the Edge of Time*

## READONATHEME: WONDER WOMEN

Top female SF authors

    Marion Zimmer Bradley, *Darkover: First Contact*
    Lois McMaster Bujold, *Cordelia's Honor*
    Suzette Haden Elgin, *Communipath Worlds*
    Mary Gentle, *Ancient Light*
    Nicola Griffith, *Ammonite*
    Gwyneth Jones, *White Queen*
    Tanith Lee, *Biting the Sun*
    Anne McCaffrey, *Restoree*
 ›› Maureen F. McHugh, *Half the Day is Night*
    Josephine Saxton, *Vector For Seven*
    Alison Sinclair, *Blueheart*
    Sherri Tepper, *The Gate to Women's Country*

# BOB SHAW (1931–96) UK

## OTHER DAYS, OTHER EYES (1972)

Alban Garrod is an engineer who has designed the windshield for a new supersonic jet. On the day of the plane's test flight, he is driving to the airfield when he is nearly involved in an accident with a sports car. Disaster is only avoided because the driver of the sports car instinctively but inexplicably slows down. When the jet's maiden flight later ends in a minor crash landing, Garrod realizes that the two accidents are linked. Both the windscreen of the automobile he encountered on the road and that of the plane are made of the same glass he has created – Thermgard. Investigating his invention, Garrod discovers that Thermgard is more than just a durable material for windows: it is *slow glass*, capable of arresting the speed of light passing through it far more than ordinary glass ever could. Eager to escape his wife's constant reminders that he is sheltering under the wing of her father's fortune, Garrod takes out a patent of his own. Slow glass will make Garrod rich and will alter the world forever, having implications for society that its inventor never imagined.

An outstanding example of a novel whose plot and characters are almost entirely driven by the affects of a unique scientific novelty (the classic >> Campbellian blueprint for traditional SF), *Other Days, Other Eyes* is a strikingly thoughtful and introspective novel. Its most elegiac section is one of the 'sidelight' stories that provide intervals in the main narrative. In it, panels of slow glass are set up in front of countryside views for years. Because of its special properties, slow glass retains images of the past and the panels can be sold as windows that will allow urban buyers to enjoy the vistas at home yet they continue to record events that are gone but not forgotten by both the farmer whose lands supply the views and his customers. Bob Shaw hailed from Northern Ireland and was the best hard SF writer in the UK during his career. Despite being very different from the New Wave authors who dominated British genre writing at the time, his best work always had the readable qualities embodied by the likes of >> John Wyndham. *Other Days, Other Eyes* is consequently essential reading not only for devotees of ideas-led SF, but for anyone who enjoys good fiction.

**≋ Read on**

*Night Walk, A Wreath of Stars*

Tom Godwin, *The Cold Equations*; Ken MacLeod, *The Human Factor*;
Alan Steele, *Orbital Decay*

# ROBERT SHECKLEY (1928–2005) USA

## IMMORTALITY INC. (1958)

Thomas Blaine is on his way home to New York from a holiday in Chesapeake Bay when he is involved in a car accident. In the last instants of his life, he realizes that he is dying so he is surprised to wake up some time later in a hospital bed. He is even more surprised to discover that, although his car accident took place in the 1950s, he is now in the year 2110. He has been snatched from the past and brought to the future by agents of the Rex Corporation, a multinational company involved in everything from reincarnation machines to spaceships. The plans Rex had for him are vetoed by Riley, the head of the company, and Blaine is turned out on to the streets of the future, his mind and soul encased in a new body. In this future, scientific facts about the afterlife and immortality have been discovered. The hereafter definitely exists but it is not open to everyone. There is inequality in death just as there is in life and only the rich get to heaven. Blaine is thrown into a strange world of would-be reincarnators, zombies who have been thrust out of their old bodies but have no new ones to inhabit and organizations like Hereafter Inc. which offer insurance deals on the afterlife.

Like a cross between ›› Kurt Vonnegut and Douglas Adams, Robert Sheckley spent more than four decades injecting a playful and blackly satiric wit into the often po-faced world of SF. Some critics would argue that his best work lies in his short stories but he wrote a number of sharply humorous novels, most notably *Journey Beyond Tomorrow*, the tale of a Polynesian Candide at large in early 21st-century America. *Immortality Inc*, originally published in a shorter form under the title *Immortality Delivered*, was Sheckley's first novel. Less overtly comic than much of Sheckley's other fiction, it remains a sophisticated and witty examination of our tangled, contradictory ideas about life, death and immortality.

### Film version: *Freejack* (1992)

### Read on

Funny SF: Douglas Adams, *Dirk Gently's Holistic Detective Agency*; Poul Anderson and Gordon R. Dickson, *Hoka! Hoka! Hoka!*; Frederic Brown, *Martians Go Home*; ›› John Sladek, *The Steam-Driven Boy*

# MARY SHELLEY (1797–1851) UK

## FRANKENSTEIN, OR THE MODERN PROMETHEUS
### (1818/1831)

In early 18th century a new variety of romantic novel appeared. The Gothic novel usually followed the formula of a young woman trapped in an old dark house or mysterious castle with an evil yet often irresistible male anti-hero, against a background of supernatural (or at least suspicious) events unfolding before a climax that disclosed some revelatory secret. In 1818, a volume sometimes categorized as a Gothic novel was published but, in reality, this was something unprecedented. It was probably the first true SF novel. In 1816 nineteen-year-old Mary Shelley, wife of the poet Percy Bysshe Shelley, penned *Frankenstein* at a villa near Geneva after a nightmare inspired by the agreement between the Shelleys, Lord Byron, his lover Claire Clairmont and his physician John Polidori to hold a ghost-story contest. The evening the competition was conceived is celebrated as one of the definitive moments in Romanticism and a milestone in the development of horror and fantasy.

*Frankenstein* depicts a post-Enlightenment rationalist hero, a scientist, who uses the new technological expertise of the Industrial Age to create a man, with the intention of improving the lot of humanity. But, like the Greek Prometheus, Frankenstein is doomed to be punished eternally for discovering the secrets of life when his creation (whom he neglects because of its monstrousness) seeks to avenge itself upon the experimenter and society. Man's disrespect for other life, the dangers of tampering with the laws of nature through technology and the subsequent disastrous events are fundamental aspects of *Frankenstein* paralleled in a vast number of SF stories published since. Radically different from (and superior to) every single film adaptation, it is a work of immense power despite being emotionally overwrought. It was revised in 1831 and both versions remain in print. Significantly, Shelley established SF as something beloved of the young and rebellious. Not only was she still a teenager when she wrote the book (later writers like ›› Brunner, ›› Silverberg and ›› Delany were similarly precocious) but she was married to a notorious atheist. She was also a woman, a woman whose mother, Mary Wollstonecraft, was the recognized founder of feminist thought. Mary Shelley herself will always be recalled as the mother of the most misunderstood monster literature ever spawned.

◣ **Significant film versions:** *Frankenstein* (1931); *The Bride of Frankenstein* (1935); *The Curse of Frankenstein* (aka *The Birth of Frankenstein*) (1957); *Frankenstein Must Be Destroyed* (1969); *Frankenstein: The True Story* (aka *Dr. Frankenstein*) (1973); *Mary Shelley's Frankenstein* (1994)

## ⮑ Read on

*The Last Man*

Proto SF (before Shelley): Giacomo Casanova, *Icosameron*; Margaret Cavendish, *The Blazing World*; Robert Paltock, *Peter Wilkins*; Jonathan Swift, *Gulliver's Travels*; Voltaire, *Micromegas*

# LUCIUS SHEPARD (b. 1947) USA

## LIFE DURING WARTIME (1987)

David Mingolla is one of thousands of US military advisers serving in insurgent Guatemala. Central America is the new Vietnam, the efficiency of Stateside troops expanded by cutting-edge stimulants and the surgically altered Psicorps, whose Air Cav division is perpetually disguised by smoked visors that are rumoured to hide their disfigurement. These flaky cowboy beserkers exert an uncomfortable fascination for Mingolla, claiming to predict the future and annihilate the enemy by thought alone. After a traumatic raid by Cuban guerrillas on Mingolla's base, the young artilleryman is trying to enjoy some R&R when one of his tense homeboys insists their squad needs to desert to evade combat casualty before losing control and being gunned down by MPs. Mingolla feels his own grip on the situation loosening when he encounters the sultry native Debora while gambling in an unusual tombola game. Drawn to the haunted soldier by his natural ESP faculty, she too states that unless Mingolla avoids the future she foresees he will die. But Mingolla's experiences only encourage him to join Psicorps and pursue an inexorable journey toward the end of the night.

Obvious parallels with *Apocalypse Now* and Joseph Conrad are entirely appropriate. *Life During Wartime* stands up beside such masterpieces because of the quality of the writing and subtle SF approach. Highly praised in broadsheet reviews when first published, it built on Shepard's reputation for the existential exploration of the soul in exotic settings – his previous work had already been compared to that of the Latin American magical realists. Despite the neotropical jungle backdrop of the book and its voluptuous prose, the book is more akin to early ›› Ballard or Céline than Márquez.

*Life During Wartime* has similarities and differences (both in content and style) to Shepard's cyberpunk contemporaries that illustrate perfectly the fecundity of 1980s' SF. Taking its title from a Talking Heads song, the book is a fearsome trip into a psychedelic heart of darkness, one that Shepard is most qualified to lead and that fans of nightmarish 'combat horror' films will eagerly follow.

### ≋ Read on

*The Jaguar Hunter*, *Kalimantan*
Angela Carter, *The Passion of New Eve*; Jorge Luis Borges, *Labyrinths*;
Geoff Ryman, *The Undiscovered Country*

## JOHN SHIRLEY (b. 1954) USA

### CITY COME A-WALKIN' (1980)

San Francisco, 2008: an urban sprawl where cash is no longer acceptable tender and the populace are threatened by Mob interference and brutal mass vigilantism. Leading face on the club scene is Stu Cole, fortyish owner of Anesthesia, a venue where computer-composed dance tracks throb mindlessly between live sets by the more authentic bands of the Angst-Rock genre. The clashing aesthetics of the two attracts a diverse clientele to Anesthesia, their hipness boosted by Stu's history as a former political lobbyist willing to challenge Bay Area corruption. One evening at his club, Cole clocks a striking, trench-coated figure standing motionless at the bar, impassive behind his shades. Cole asks Catz, a mildly telepathic singer with the night's band, to scan the individual for information. Conveying sense-impressions through improvised song lyrics, Catz spits out a number entitled *City Come A-Walkin'*, indicating to Cole that the implacable stranger is nothing less than a materialized avatar of San Francisco itself. A gestalt entity borne of the merged will and energy of human minds and machines, this being can only be called one thing – City. As Cole follows City into the night to witness the reality of Catz's claim, he takes a stand alongside the merciless might of the metropolis itself with the intention of righting the wrongs that have blighted the streets which are its veins.

Gritty, gleaming and impassioned, *City Come A-Walkin'* is acknow-ledged by ›› William Gibson as the immediate precursor (or possibly the seminal work) of the cyberpunk school. Combining the influence of poetic alt.rock icons like Patti Smith with prescient visions of the coming IT era, this is one of several vivid, heartfelt novels of attitude from Shirley – who fronted several Californian bands himself – to feature punk characters. Best known for his screenplay for *The Crow*, Shirley has also written some alarming horror novels that complement his steely, methedrine-laced SF.

## ⮂ Read on

*A Song Called Youth* (a trilogy about a dystopian future which consists of *Eclipse*, *Eclipse Penumbra* and *Eclipse Corona*)

Rock 'n' Roll lifestyles: ›› Brian Aldiss, *Brothers of the Head*; ›› William Gibson, *Idoru*; Lewis Shiner, *Slam*; ›› Norman Spinrad, *Little Heroes*

# LISTEN ON A THEME SCIENCE FICTION ROCK AND ROLL

SF has influenced popular music since the fifties, from early rockabilly songs about flying saucers to contemporary dance music using samples from SF television shows. Because of the popularity of SF novels in 1960s/1970s counterculture and the arrival of the synthesizer, this was the golden age of 'space rock' in genres as diverse as psychedelia, glam, progressive, punk, funk and electronica. The albums selected here contain some of the best-articulated SF themes in popular music to date.

David Bowie, *The Rise and Fall of Ziggy Stardust and the Spiders From Mars* (1972) (Five years before doomsday, an extraterrestrial rock singer seeks stardom on Earth)

David Bowie, *Diamond Dogs* (1974) (>> Orwell's *Nineteen Eighty-Four* merges with >> Ellison's 'A Boy and His Dog' in this glam rock masterwork)

Robert Calvert, *Lucky Leif and the Longships* (1975) (How would popular music have been affected if the Vikings' attempts to colonize America had succeeded?)

Hawkwind, *Epocheclipse* (3 CD edition, collected 1999) (A definitive anthology from the psychedelic group who habitually base songs on the works of SF writers)

Paul Kantner's Jefferson Starship, *(It's A Fresh Wind That) Blows Against the Empire* (1970) (Outcasts hijack a spaceship to escape a dystopian society in this acid rock favourite)

Kraftwerk, *The Man Machine* (1978) (Germany's synthesizer kings celebrate robots, space travel, cyborgs and the futuristic city)

Parliament, *Motor Booty Affair* (1978) (Funk music reaches the undersea city of Atlantis with groovy consequences)

Rush, *2112* (1976) (Canadian progressive metal band depicts a future where music is banned until a solitary rebel finds an ancient electric guitar)

The Stranglers, *The Meninblack* (1980) (The top punk band eerily investigate alien intervention in humanity's evolution many years before the film *Men in Black* is conceived)

Jeff Wayne/various artists, *The Musical Version of the War of the Worlds* (1978) (Thrillingly dramatizes the **»** Wells classic in spoken word, songs, music and sound effects)

# ROBERT SILVERBERG (b. 1935) USA

## THE MAN IN THE MAZE (1969)

Dick Muller lives alone on the planet Lemnos, in an archaic maze city abandoned millennia before by its former inhabitants. An exile by choice, Muller's historic first contact with the extraterrestrial Hydrans ended in calamity when their alterations of his body chemistry transformed him into a pariah. No one can stand to be near Muller, for all the dark aspects of his soul can be sensed by men, his consciousness perpetually projecting the psychic equivalent of a foul stench. Muller learns to survive amid the automatic traps and myriads of other dangers that still haunt the city, protected from further contact with his fellow humans.

Earth's interstellar empire needs aid: a civilization of giant organisms is expanding its colonies into Terran space and all attempts to establish communication with the aliens has failed. Charles Boardman leads an expedition to Lemnos where he will send callow youth Ned Rawlins into the deadly maze to make contact with Muller. Rawlins will have to negotiate the traps, endure the vileness of Muller's affliction and trick the banished one into emerging from the labyrinth to take on the challenge of opening a dialogue with the new extraterrestrial menace.

Silverberg produced numerous novels and stories before diversifying into non-fiction, where his commercial success was remarkable. In the late sixties he returned to SF and began producing his most accomplished work: although many critics cite *Thorns* (1967) as the beginning of a decade's work which saw him write his masterpieces, we believe the *The Man in the Maze* to be his first magnum opus. The tight plotting and moral message of the book (typical of the burnished sharpness of Silverberg's best work) combine the 'sense of wonder' of traditional SF with the literary attack of the New Wave. With a magnificent command of character that bravely embraces unsympathetic protagonists and a mature understanding of human motivation, Silverberg's sometimes detached style allowed him to conquer such difficult themes as power, guilt, redemption and transcendence with a confidence only the best novelists can achieve.

## 🐟 Read on

Silverberg's major works: *Nightwings*, *Downward to the Earth*, *A Time of Changes*, *The Book of Skulls*, *Dying Inside*

John Boyd, *The Last Starship From Earth*; >> Philip K. Dick, *The Penultimate Truth*; >> Norman Spinrad, *Agent of Chaos*

## JOHN SLADEK (1937–2000) USA

### TIK-TOK (1983)

The narrator of Sladek's blackly satirical novel is the robot, Tik-Tok, whose malfunctioning 'asimov circuits' have turned him into an amoral psychopath. Tik-Tok records his life from his first job as a domestic servant in the Deep South, through the murders and mischief he commits on his way to wealth and power, to his final ambiguous comeuppance. In a gleeful reversal of expectations, *Tik-Tok* provides the flipside to Sladek's earlier two-part novel about a thinking machine called Roderick. Where Roderick is an innocent abroad, wandering wide-eyed through the dubious wonders of American civilization, Tik-Tok is a malevolent Machiavellian, prepared to manipulate both fellow robots and human beings in his relentless pursuit of his own ends. Far from proving a handicap, his amorality propels him to the top of American society, even into the vice-presidency.

John Sladek was one of the wittiest and most original SF writers of his generation. Born in America but resident for many years in England, where he was linked with the writers of the British New Wave, he displayed his playful and parodic imagination in a number of quirky and offbeat novels. *Tik-Tok* shows Sladek at his most slyly inventive, appropriating characters and ideas from classic American fantasy and

SF and using them for his own purposes. The villainous robot anti-hero shares his name with a faithful mechanical servant in L. Frank Baum's Oz books; the entire plot subverts the famous Three Laws of Robotics used in ➤➤ Asimov's fiction from the 1940s and 1950s and reveals how flawed their relative optimism might prove. In the real world of the future the relationship between man and machine might not be one of benign symbiosis but of bitter competition. *Tik-Tok* is tough-minded satire written by an author who has often been compared to ➤➤ Kurt Vonnegut in his bleak playfulness and wry perspective on the world.

### ☙ Read on
*The Complete Roderick* (compilation volume of Sladek's two books, *Roderick* and *Roderick at Random,* in which a well-meaning robot inadvertently causes disaster through his child-like innocence of the world), *The Reproductive System*
Marc Laidlaw, *Dad's Nuke;* ➤➤ Robert Sheckley, *Options;* ➤➤ Kurt Vonnegut, *Slapstick or Lonesome No More*

# CORDWAINER SMITH (1913–66) USA

NORSTRILIA (collected 1975)
What happens when a US Army Intelligence operative takes time out from producing a seminal text on psychological warfare to pen some SF? The answer is intoxicating and sometimes pleasantly baffling. Old North Australia is a bleak globe colonized by Antipodean sheep farmers.

The ewes on Norstrilia are monstrous in size, afflicted by a disease that yields a useful by-product, a compound called Stroon, which conveys great longevity upon the user. Consequently, Norstrilia is the richest planet in the universe. Maintaining their sense of perspective by taxing themselves to the hilt and employing a rigorous system of self-culling to keep their immortal population in check, the humble shepherds dwell in homely rustic simplicity. Despite his almost non-existent telepathic quotient, Rod McBann escapes the cull and tends to his flock. Partially ostracized by Norstrilian society and threatened by an offworld official with a grudge, Rod consults his antique computer for advice. But his family heirloom is no ordinary AI, but a mechanical maverick that contrives a stratagem allowing Rod to buy the Earth and become the wealthiest being in the cosmos. On a sojourn to the home-world which is undergoing a cultural revolution called The Rediscovery of Mankind, Rod becomes involved in the conflict between the Underpeople (genetically enhanced animals) and the Instrumentality, the omnipotent government of humanity itself.

Constructed from short stories published years earlier, *Norstrilia* is the hub of Smith's *Instrumentality of Mankind* sequence, which includes the majority of his work. In an unsettling sing-song style believed to derive from the authors' extensive knowledge of oriental languages, Smith dispensed with blatant infodump (the often cumbersome explanatory sections common in SF stories that used to be thought essential to clarify the background of the tale), letting the reader piece together his detailed and complex macroverse. Smith's influence is notable upon writers as diverse as >> Silverberg and >> Bayley and his unique style continues to entertain readers with a penchant for the whimsical and surprising.

## ⮒ Read on

*The Rediscovery of Man*, *The Instrumentality of Mankind*
Australian SF: Russell Braddon, *The Year of the Angry Rabbit*; Damien
Broderick, *Godplayers*; George Turner, *The Sea and Summer*

## E.E. 'DOC' SMITH (1890–1965) USA

### TRIPLANETARY (1948)

Drawing on material first published in the 1930s, *Triplanetary* is the first
(chronologically) in Smith's sequence of 'Lensmen' books, the one
which establishes the back-story behind his epic saga of intergalactic
warfare. Billions of years in the past, a struggle began between the
malign, power-hungry Eddorians and the peaceful, benevolent Arisians.
Life on Earth itself is a consequence of this confrontation, since the
Arisians chose to seed those planets in the universe capable of
sustaining life as part of their programme to defeat the Eddorians, and
the history of mankind, from the fall of Atlantis and the reign of the
Roman Emperors to the 20th-century world wars and beyond, is deeply
(although obliviously) implicated in the conflict between the two
superior races. As *Triplanetary* unfolds, the action moves into the
future and the new age when mankind has begun to reach out to the
stars and to meet with alien races.

A food scientist who is reported to have been the inventor of the
process for sticking powdered sugar to doughnuts, Smith began publishing his stories in the pulp magazines of the 1920s and he is usually

considered the founding father of 'space opera'. By no standards known to man (or, in all probability, alien) can Smith be regarded as a subtle or sophisticated writer but the sheer, rollicking energy of his sagas and the inventiveness with which he peopled his millennia-spanning narratives are enormously engaging. The future technologies he creates are ingenious (indeed, in some instances, have proved surprisingly prescient) and his characters, pasteboard though they sometimes seem, are none the less remarkably memorable. His influence on SF in other media, from the *Star Wars* films to computer games, has been long-lasting and still continues. For all his limitations (he did not write what even the most generous critic could call great literature), Smith remains a major and unignorable figure in the history of the genre.

### ≋ Read on

*The Skylark of Space*

›› Isaac Asimov, *The Stars Like Dust*; A.A. Attanasio, *Radix*; Gordon R. Dickson, *Soldier Ask Not*; E.C. Tubb, *The Winds of Gath*

# NORMAN SPINRAD (b. 1940) USA

## THE IRON DREAM (1972)

Reading *The Iron Dream* is a unique experience. You open it, flicking past the title page, finding a plot blurb, bibliography and a potted author biography, none of which relate to Spinrad. You turn another leaf, finding another title page, bearing the legend *Lord of the Swastika by Adolf Hitler.* It appears that a different book has been concealed within the binding of ***The Iron Dream***, but this is no printer's error. You have entered an alternative history, not one where the Axis won the Second World War but one where Hitler quit radical politics in the twenties and emigrated to the USA, where he became a pulp writer while the Soviet Union expanded, instigating an anti-semitic holocaust. Then you settle down to enjoy Hitler's final classic, written shortly before his death in 1954. *Lord of the Swastika* is set in a post-atomic future, when Europe is peopled by radioactive mutants and threatened by the evil eastern empire of the Dominators of Zind, a race of telepathic collectivists bent on world conquest. Enter Feric Jaggar, a racially perfect human who yearns to purge Earth of its inferior genetic aberrations. To this end Feric recruits an elite Aryan corps of forest-dwelling biker barbarians to his cause, convincing them of his right to dominion by wielding the mystical Truncheon of Held, the ancestral symbol of his pure-blooded people. Feric goes on to fulfil his destiny as his Knights of the Swastika take their campaign to Zind itself.

   Writing to counter the right-wing tendency that had been present in SF since ❯❯ Campbell took over editorship of ***Astounding***, Spinrad aimed for the jugular of fascism itself, illustrating its pathological obsessions in prose that is a superb parody of infantile, wish-fulfilment sci-fi and macho sword and sorcery. This rip-roaring, startlingly original read is as polemical as it is funny, typical of the direct approach of an author no stranger to controversy. Spinrad's previous book, ***Bug Jack Barron*** (serialized in ***New Worlds***) prompted questions in Parliament when an MP's complaint about the novel's four-letter words resulted in the magazine's Arts Council grant being suspended and a ban by W.H.

Smith. Since then the author has continued writing blunt and uncompromising novels of attitude that established him as a New Wave icon while inspiring the cyberpunk generation.

### ≋ Read on

*A World Between*, *The Void Captain's Tale*

Questionable messiahs: ›› Philip K. Dick, *The Three Stigmata of Palmer Eldritch*; ›› Robert A. Heinlein, *Stranger in a Strange Land*; ›› Roger Zelazny, *Isle of the Dead*

# NEAL STEPHENSON (b. 1959) USA

## SNOW CRASH (1992)

Near-future America has disintegrated from a nation state to a patchwork quilt of retailing franchises (run by organizations like the Mafia), gated estates known as 'burbclaves', multi-lane freeways and vast airports. Those who can, spend long periods of time in virtual reality. In the real world, Stephenson's hero/protagonist, the Nipponese-American Hiro Protagonist, is a pizza delivery boy turned part-time intel hacker and concert promoter; in the Metaverse, the vast virtual reality domain where millions hang out via their computers, Hiro is one of the kings of the castle, a master samurai swordsman who wrote much of the code on which the Metaverse runs. While hanging out at The Black Sun, the Metaverse's coolest club, he is offered a new cyber-drug called

Snow Crash and is soon plunged into a surreal world where billionaire businessmen plot domination of both reality and the Metaverse and flotillas of refugees from Asia head for the shores of California. His only ally amid the madness seems to be Y.T., a teenage skateboarding courier who rides the freeways by harpooning passing cars and dragging herself along in their wakes.

Précis-defying in its plot, *Snow Crash* takes such apparently diverse subjects as the philosophy of computing, Sumerian mythology, Biblical criticism, conspiracy theories, medical virology and linguistics and weaves them into a hectic narrative of pursuit and paranoia. Owing as much to the post-modern fiction of writers like Thomas Pynchon and Don DeLillo as it does to cyberpunk SF, Stephenson's novel is a book that takes all the ideas about the internet and virtual reality current in the early 1990s and projects them into a weird future of his own imagining. Very funny and wildly energetic, it is an exceptional novel. Stephenson continues to write highly challenging and inventive fiction, both inside and outside the SF genre, but he has still not surpassed *Snow Crash* for sheer originality and dazzle.

## ⪦ Read on

*The Diamond Age, Cryptonomicon*
Postmodern SF: ›› William S. Burroughs, *The Wild Boys*; ›› William Gibson, *Virtual Light*; Larry McCaffrey (ed.), *Storming the Reality Studio*; David Ohle, *Motorman*

# BRUCE STERLING (b. 1954) USA

## INVOLUTION OCEAN (1977)

Drug addict John Newhouse lives on the colonized world Nullaqua, making his living and sustaining a habit by dealing to friends on the planet Reverie. Newhouse's poison is a narco-psychedelic called Syncophine ('Flare' to its users) distilled from an oil derived from a species of whale that lives only in the bizarre Nullaquan ocean, a sea that is comprised not of water, but of dust. When galactic confederacy laws encourage the Nullaquan government to start cracking down on users of Flare, Newhouse's supplies are cut off and his fellow-addicts manoeuvre him into signing on as able seaman on a whaling ship captained by the flamboyant Nils Desperandum. While learning the secrets of Nullaqua on an unforgettable voyage, Newhouse falls into a bizarre sado-masochistic relationship with the ship's lookout, the winged extraterrestrial woman named Dalusa...

>> Harlan Ellison discovered the original version of the book at a writer's workshop and bought it for his *Discovery* series. Sterling expanded his novelette and the rest is history: by the early eighties Sterling was one of the key architects of the cyberpunk movement. Although Sterling has written technically superior novels, his first book remains the most memorable due to the sheer originality and utter strangeness of the world he created. The surface of Nullaqua is uninhabitable, bearing no atmosphere except in the 500-mile diameter, 70-mile deep crater that houses the ocean of dust and the port towns dotted around it. Descendants of a puritanical religious sect, the human inhabitants of the planet have grown thick mats of hair in their noses and bushy brows and eyelashes to protect their lungs from the dust,

while the alien sea is teeming with exotic and deadly life-forms. This superbly realized setting will impress anyone who relished the impressive world-building of *Dune* but was daunted by the length of that epic while the vivid, decadent characters and convincing descriptions of drug use, clearly influenced by the counterculture of the sixties, will appeal to readers who identify with rebellious and romantic anti-heroes.

## ⮂ Read on
*The Artificial Kid*
Bizarre biospheres: ►► Brian Aldiss, *Helliconia Spring*; Piers Anthony, *Omnivore*; Joan Slonczewski, *A Door Into Ocean*; Robert Charles Wilson, *Bios*

# GEORGE R. STEWART (1895–1980) USA

## EARTH ABIDES (1949)
Most stories of a post-catastrophe planet Earth posit a nuclear holocaust from which the survivors emerge to stumble across a ravaged, irradiated landscape. By contrast, George R. Stewart's novel, his only venture into science fiction, takes place in the aftermath of a mysterious plague which has all but destroyed humanity. His hero, Isherwood Williams, returns from a journey into the wilderness to find that he has the continent almost to himself. Nearly everyone else is dead and it is only after a long period of solitary roaming through the

devastated towns and cities of America that he finds a female survivor whom he wishes to marry. Stewart's novel charts, with great simplicity and conviction, the generations that grow up around Ish. As the years pass, the memories of the pre-plague world fade and the extended family members live more and more like America's original indigenous population. In choosing the name 'Ish' for his protagonist, Stewart was deliberately echoing the accounts of Ishi, sole survivor of a tribe of a Native Americans whom anthropologists encountered in California in the years immediately before the First World War. Just as Ishi was witness to the disappearance of the world of his forefathers, so too does Isherwood Williams see the civilization he remembers drift into legend or oblivion. His grandchildren and great-grandchildren revere him but the pre-plague world he knew has gone.

George R. Stewart was a polymath and academic whose interests ranged from the history of American place names to meteorology and natural history. He wrote a number of novels, of which *Earth Abides* is the best-known and the only one that can be plausibly described as SF. In its profound and prescient concerns for ecology and the environment and in its memorable vision of a world in which 'men go and come, but Earth abides', the book more than deserves the classic status it now has.

### ☙ Read on

》 J.G. Ballard, *The Wind From Nowhere*; John Christopher, *The Death of Grass*; 》 D.G. Compton, *The Silent Multitude*; Michael Coney, *Winter's Children*; Peter Dickinson, *The Weathermonger*

# ARKADY STRUGATKSY (1925–91)
# BORIS STRUGATSKY (b. 1931) Russia

## ROADSIDE PICNIC (1972)

The Visitors come unannounced, stay only for a short while and leave without fanfare. Their passage is marked in six places. These areas are shunned, lethal to mankind and sealed off by the authorities. They are known simply as the Zones.

Thirty years later, when scientific establishments have been built adjacent to each Zone, the mysteries of the Visitors remain. Many have expired in the Zones while attempting to recover the technological detritus the Visitors left behind, killed by unearthly gravitational effects, deadly magnetic traps and other indefinable menaces, which defy scientific knowledge. Despite all efforts to prevent civilians from venturing into the Zones, a tradition of exploration, discovery and retrieval has developed. The men known only as Stalkers brave the Zones in their search for alien artefacts to sell on the black market, growing wise in their understanding of these visited areas, navigating them with respect and grace. Redrick Schuhart is a rogueish Stalker who defies the bullets of the border guards time and again to negotiate the wonders and snares of the Zone in Harmont, Canada to loot the most valuable booty of all times: something that will confer a man's deepest wish upon him, no matter what it may be.

The Strugatsky brothers were the most acclaimed speculative writers in Russia, typifying the traditions of European SF, being exponents of the literary experimentalism and spiky characterization of their precursors. Benefiting from a positive critical reception in the West from the mid-seventies onward, when their works first appeared in translation, they are best known by association with the cinema adaptation of *Roadside Picnic* by Andrei Tarkovsky, who also filmed the original version of ›› Lem's *Solaris*. *Roadside Picnic* is an entrancing amalgam of lively 'sense of wonder' genre elements and the witty, absurdist heaviness of the very best continental literature that both fans of classic SF and European modernism will enjoy.

◀ **Film version:** *Stalker* (1979, Russia)

❧ **Read on**
*Prisoners of Power*
European SF: Pierre Boulle (France), *Planet of the Apes*; Mikhail Bulgakov (Russia), *The Fatal Eggs*; Knut Faldbakken (Norway), *Twilight Country*; Boris Vian (France), *The Froth on the Daydream*

# THEODORE STURGEON (1918–85) USA

## MORE THAN HUMAN (1953)
*More Than Human*, a book that ›› James Blish once called 'one of the very few authentic masterpieces science fiction can boast', takes an array of ideas about psychology and the potential abilities of the mind that were current at the time it was written and uses them to suggest what the next stage of human evolution might be. In a three-part

narrative, Sturgeon traces the progress of a group of outcasts and misfits – including an idiot boy with telepathic powers called Lone, black twins with telekinetic abilities and a severely retarded child who possesses hidden mental gifts – as they gradually unite to form a gestalt being which transcends ordinary humanity. Lone's death and his replacement by the orphan Gerry, prepared to kill to maintain the group's integrity, is followed by the arrival of Hip Barrows, whose coming makes the gestalt complete and leads it to the discovery that it is not entirely alone.

Like so many of the best SF novels of the 1950s, *More Than Human* began as a series of short stories (first published in *Galaxy* magazine) and its origins do show. Ironically, for a work which shows how a group of individuals become greater than the sum of their parts when brought together, the stories do not always meld as smoothly as they could but the reader is carried through the patchwork narrative by the power of Sturgeon's imagination and the subtlety of his prose. The slow emergence of Lone from his almost vegetable state to an awareness of the world around him and his own responses to the people in it is a particularly vivid and intensely imagined piece of writing. Always prepared to tackle ideas and themes that less adventurous genre writers of the period ignored, Sturgeon's fiction shows just how American SF grew in sophistication and ambitiousness in the early years of the 1950s.

### 🕮 Read on

*To Marry Medusa*
Nancy Kress, *Beggars in Spain*; Edgar Pangborn, *Davy*; ›› Keith Roberts, *The Inner Wheel*; ›› A.E. Van Vogt, *Slan*; ›› John Wyndham, *The Chrysalids*

# MICHAEL SWANWICK (b. 1950) USA

## STATIONS OF THE TIDE (1991)

The distant future. Earth has been ruined by the misuse of science. On the colonized worlds, advanced technology and innovation are prohibited to prevent history repeating itself. On Miranda, a world seasonally engulfed by immense tides that drown much of the planet as its icecaps rapidly melt, a trickster named Gregorian is offering the locals the promise of being transformed into amphibians, allowing them to avoid the evacuations that precede the coming of the ocean. The Bureaucrat hails from the Floating Worlds, artificial space-borne environments where cutting-edge science is permitted. His mission is to find and apprehend Gregorian, who is charged with using banned technology. Making landfall on Miranda, the Bureaucrat weaves a serpentine path through the steamy, superstitious, many-hued culture that resembles New Orleans during a perpetual Mardi Gras, accompanied by his briefcase, an artificial intelligence that patches him into the Puzzle Palace, a virtual reality construct where the Bureaucrat and his colleagues hold conference. On the way he will be tutored in secret sexual lore, poisoned by alien hallucinogens, suffer and anticipate tortuous double-crosses. Leading the Bureaucrat on is Gregorian, who may be toying with him in a Godgame as perverse and exotic as the denizens of Miranda itself.

Densely complex and multi-faceted, *Stations of the Tide* shows just why Swanwick is one of the most popular SF writers of the past fifteen years. Winner of numerous awards, he boldly combines the contemporary concerns of radical hard SF with a lush palette of imagery redolent of the best fantasy writing. Seasoned with light Shakespearian allusion, *Stations* is a kaleidoscope of juxtapositions, where television vies with sorcery and the matter-of-fact-dryness of the Bureaucrat contrasts vividly with his explicit carnal escapades and calm confidence in dealing with the villainous Gregorian.

## ☙ Read on

*In the Drift, Vacuum Flowers*
Colourful humanist SF worlds: **>>** Maureen F. McHugh, *Nekropolis*; Paul Park, *Coelestis*; Sherri Tepper, *Grass*

# WALTER TEVIS (1928–84) USA

## THE MAN WHO FELL TO EARTH (1963)

Stumbling across a new brand of high-resolution self-developing film that defies conventional photochemistry, Professor Nathan Bryce decides it is time for a change. Bored with academia, he seeks out a position with the firm that manufactures the film, a bold company called World Enterprises Corporation whose revolutionary patents are transforming American technology. Bryce is recruited to work on a space probe project WEC is developing, fuelling his suspicion that the head of the business, the reclusive Thomas Jerome Newton, may be more than just an eccentric genius. Bryce is correct: Newton is a disguised humanoid from the planet Anthea, a world dying from lack of resources and the impact of numerous wars. Newton's objective to save the few surviving Antheans while preventing the human race from embarking on disastrous nuclear conflicts is hampered by many obstacles – for it is not only the alien's body that is weakened on Earth, but his sanity. Newton finds that indolence and alcohol have begun to overwhelm him as easily as they have enslaved Betty Jo, a sentimental middle-aged lush he encounters by chance. Bryce, Newton and Betty Jo's inexorable slide into ennui could spell the end of not one but two worlds.

Furnishing chilling insights into what it would be like to be alone, frightened and frail on a strange planet, Tevis's elegant, painstaking creation of Anthean physiology and culture make this book far more stimulating than scores of other more conventional invasion narratives, resulting in an exciting, slow-burning novel whose calm grip tightens on the reader like a constrictor. Despite publishing short stories in the magazines, Tevis reads like a mainstream writer. *The Man Who Fell to Earth* is his crowning achievement, proof that pure genre-based fiction can be written with the elegance of contemporary literature while retaining the energy such attempts often lose. An English literature professor whose relationship with drinking was difficult, Tevis admitted that much of his fiction was autobiographical, perhaps explaining why Newton's alienation is so profoundly observed in this outstanding novel.

◀ **Film version:** *The Man Who Fell to Earth* (1976)

≋ **Read on**
*Jeremy Reed, The Diamond Nebula*
The (Un)sympathetic other: ➤➤ Brian Aldiss, *The Dark Light Years*; Gardner Dozois, *Strangers*; Damon Knight, *The Man in the Tree*; ➤➤ Theodore Sturgeon, *Venus Plus X*

# A.E. VAN VOGT (1912–2000) Canada/USA

## THE VOYAGE OF THE SPACE BEAGLE (1950)

A space ship is on a long, exploratory journey, travelling from the Earth into the deepest reaches of space. During the voyage the crew members come into contact with a succession of largely hostile aliens – an intelligent cat-like creature with telepathic abilities, a monstrous and malevolent being that floats in space and attempts to hitch a ride on the passing Space Beagle – and conduct their own internal struggle for power between the advocates of traditional science and the exponents of a new philosophy called Nexialism. First published in book form in 1950, *The Voyage of the Space Beagle* was fashioned out of several stories Van Vogt had published years earlier and its origin is revealed in the episodic nature of its plot. Each of the encounters with aliens is almost self-contained, as the space explorers learn again and again that the new worlds they discover pose disturbing threats and challenges to their mission.

Most of Van Vogt's best work was done by 1950 but his influence on the genre continued long after the publication of *The Voyage of the Space Beagle*. Many other writers, most notably ›› Philip K. Dick, went on record to say how much they owed to him and his uncredited impact on SF in movies and on TV has been considerable. The basic idea behind *Star Trek* (the spaceship boldly going where no man has been before) clearly takes something from the journey of the Space Beagle and two of the short stories later used in constructing the novel were the basis for the film *Alien*, a fact the movie-makers eventually acknowledged by settling out of court a lawsuit Van Vogt brought against them. In his pioneering vision and inventiveness, Van Vogt was (with

>> Heinlein and >> Asimov) one of the greatest of Golden Age writers and bold, galaxy-spanning stories like *The Voyage of the Space Beagle* still stimulate the reader's imagination.

### 🕮 Read on
*The World of Null-A, Slan, The Weapon Shops of Isher*
>> Robert A. Heinlein, *Star Beast*; L. Ron Hubbard, *Fear*; Colin Wilson, *The Mind Parasites*

# JACK VANCE (b. 1916) USA

## THE LANGUAGES OF PAO (1958)

When Panarch Panasper is apparently assassinated by his son Beran during a tense meeting with offworld traders from Mercantile, the culturally sedate planet Pao is plunged into turmoil. Beran's uncle Bustamonte becomes Regent until the lad is mature enough to become Panarch, while the boy himself is spirited away to Breakness, a world dominated by the Wizards of the Institute, humans whose cunning intellects are matched only by the cybernetic augmentation that makes them supermen. Under the wing of Institute Wizard Palofax, Beran grows to manhood while studying linguistics. But Pao is easily bested by raiders from the planet Batmarsh and is forced to pay a hefty annual tribute to their martial conquerors. Seeking advice from Breakness, Bustamonte falls for the machinations of Palofax, who has his own designs on Pao. Palofax believes a new breed of Paonese is required –

effective warriors and technicians. To achieve this, aggressive new languages are engineered, unleashing the scientific and military tendencies latent in the Paonese, whose subdued character was dictated by the muted structure of their homeworld's tongue. Meanwhile, Beran has plans of his own for Pao...

As well as the colourful, elegant usage of words typical of Vance's style, this novel displays the author's passion for language by employing a plot structure powered by the idea of vocabulary as humankind's means of progress. Despite the high concept nature of the story, *The Languages of Pao* is no arid, academic read; it's a swift-moving interplanetary intrigue with elements of quasi-Renaissance imperialism admirers of *Dune* or *Star Wars* will enjoy, and the pages turn easily and rapidly. Vance has long been regarded as creator of some of the finest planetary romances and 'dying Earth' fantasies in the annals of genre writing. His genius for coining memorable and plausible nouns for unearthly beings and artefacts is displayed at its very best here, in one of the earliest SF novels to focus on linguistics. Although it is less florid than some of his better-known works, *The Languages of Pao* is a clever, original adventure story and a shimmering example of Vance's verbal and world-building skills.

## ≋ Read on

*The Dragon Masters*, *Emphyrio*
Linguistics: ➤➤ Samuel R. Delany, *Babel 17*; Suzette Haden Elgin, *Native Tongue*; ➤➤ Ian Watson, *The Embedding*

# JULES VERNE (1828 –1905) France

## JOURNEY TO THE CENTRE OF THE EARTH (1864)

When Jules Verne began writing in the 1860s, explorers were regularly returning from the world's furthest flung places with stories of the wonders they had seen and their books became bestsellers. In the same decades as they published their astonishing narratives, science and progress seemed unstoppable in their benevolent march towards a better future. Verne's genius was to take his travellers one step further into that future. His books often read very much like the memoirs of real-life explorers of his day but his heroes, rather than merely shedding light on Darkest Africa, are riding rockets to the moon, descending into the Earth's core or living perpetually beneath the seas.

*Journey to the Centre of the Earth* is the story of the adventures of Professor Lidenbrock, an eccentric and irascible German geologist, and his nephew Axel, the narrator of the novel. Tucked inside an ancient Icelandic manuscript, the professor finds a cryptic note written by a 16th-century alchemist named Arne Saknussemm. Once deciphered, the note tells of a supposed journey Saknussemm made into the crater of an extinct volcano. Determined to repeat the alchemist's intra-terrestrial voyage, Lidenbrock immediately drags his unwilling nephew off to Iceland where, together with a phlegmatic guide named Hans, they descend into the crater of Mount Sneffels. There they discover a world of wonders hidden beneath the Earth's surface. A vast underground sea harbours marine reptiles long extinct elsewhere. Launched on a perilous raft journey across the sea, the explorers eventually find evidence to suggest that prehistoric animals and early races of man still flourish in the underground world. Verne draws on contemporary notions that the Earth might be hollow, theories that had not been wholly discredited at the time he was writing, to fashion an exciting narrative of adventure and scientific speculation.

### 🐝 Read on

*Twenty Thousand Leagues Under the Sea, From the Earth to the Moon, Paris in the Twentieth Century* (a strange and intriguing novel, not published until decades after Verne's death, in which he speculates about the French capital in 1960, a city where business and technology have triumphed over culture and the fine arts)

Edward Bellamy, *Looking Backward 2000–1887*; Edward Bulwer-Lytton, *The Coming Race* (aka *Vril*); H. Rider Haggard, *She*; Edgar Allan Poe, *The Science Fiction of Edgar Allen Poe*; Mark Twain, *A Connecticut Yankee in King Arthur's Court*

# VERNOR VINGE (b. 1944) USA

## A FIRE UPON THE DEEP (1992)

In Vinge's vast vision of a universe in which different zones of space impose their different constraints on technological development (in the 'slow' zone, faster-than-light travel is impossible but other zones have no such restriction), a long dormant and evil power is accidentally released with devastating consequences. The only potentially effective counter-measure to this Blight sweeping through galaxies lies with two children marooned in an alien world, medieval in its civilization, where the dominant creatures, the Tines, come from a dog-like species that only gains its intelligence when it combines in packs. A mission to rescue the children and take possession of the counter-measure, led by an enhanced and millennia-old human named Pham Nuwen, races across space, pursued by all those who have a vested interest in the spread of the Blight. Meanwhile, on the planet of the Tines, the children are caught up in a power struggle between two rival clans.

Vernor Vinge is a mathematician and computer scientist who taught for many years in San Diego State University and, outside the SF world, he is well-known for his ideas about the future growth of technology and what he called, in an essay published only a year after *A Fire Upon the Deep*, 'the coming technological singularity'. The singularity is the moment at which, in Vinge's own words, 'we will have the technological means to create superhuman intelligence'. Shortly after that, again according to Vinge, 'the human era will be ended'. His epic novel clearly reflects his ideas – many of the beings in *A Fire Upon the Deep* live in a post-singularity universe – but it is also an unabashed and enthralling example of contemporary space opera. It is a book in which unfettered speculation about future technology and a more old-fashioned delight in the creation of alien worlds combine to brilliant effect.

## ≋ Read on

*A Deepness in the Sky* (Vinge's prequel to *A Fire Upon the Deep*, set in the same universe but 30,000 years earlier), *Across Realtime*, *The True Names and Other Dangers*

Communication: Stephen Donaldson, *The Gap into Conflict: The Real Story*; ›› Larry Niven and Jerry Pournelle, *The Mote in God's Eye*; Naomi

Mitchison, *Memoirs of a Spacewoman*; Mike Resnick, *Santiago*; Spider and Jeanette Robinson, *Stardance*

# KURT VONNEGUT (b. 1922) USA

## SLAUGHTERHOUSE-FIVE (1969)

Billy Pilgrim is a mild-mannered middle-class optometrist from New York State. The sole survivor of a charter-plane crash, he begins speaking in public about the close encounter of the third kind he experienced. Abducted in a flyer saucer by laughable BEMS (bug eyed monsters), Billy claims he was exhibited naked in the equivalent of a zoo on the planet Tralfamadore, accompanied by a luscious movie starlet called Montana Wildhack. Pilgrim's psychological arrow of time has disintegrated and now resembles that of the Tralfamadorians. Instead of perceiving chronology as flowing in the direction of the thermodynamic arrow, Billy is involuntarily shuttled back and forth between different episodes in his life, most notably the period he spent as a naive young GI during the Second World War. In December 1944, when his unit is captured by the Wehrmacht, Billy is led into the ornate, fairytale city of Dresden, the most exquisite place he has ever seen. He experiences at first hand the asinine folly of war and the arbitrary nature of fate when the city is razed by the most brutal incendiary bombing in history. While the firestorm rages, Billy and his companions, good and evil, shelter in the cellars beneath the abattoir in which they are billeted.

When they emerge it is to desolation that only his dialogues with the philosophically inclined Tralfamadorians will allow him to endure.

Based on his own experience of wartime Dresden, *Slaughterhouse-Five* was the witty, sardonic and wise book that made Vonnegut an international literary bestseller. His sophisticated, ironic style – warm, shoulder-shrugging, misanthropic yet hopeful – has long been critically admired, dextrously employing speculative ideas as plangent metaphors for the eternal absurdities of the inhuman condition. Although his early SF novels *The Sirens of Titan* and *Cat's Cradle* are his purest works, *Slaughterhouse-Five* reveals Vonnegut at the pinnacle of his interdisciplinary standing, encompassing the gleeful energy of genre SF and the knowing perspective of mainstream satire. His attachment to SF is embodied by Kilgore Trout, a screwball-savant sci-fi hack who often operates as Vonnegut's sagacious mouthpiece in several of his other hilarious, humanitarian novels.

📖 **Film version:** *Slaughterhouse-Five* (1972)

📚 **Read on**
*Galapagos*
Homages to Vonnegut's early work: Douglas Adams, *The Hitch-Hiker's Guide to the Galaxy*; Kilgore Trout (>> Philip José Farmer), *Venus on the Half-Shell*
Time reversals: Martin Amis, *Time's Arrow*; >> Philip K. Dick, *Counter-Clock World*

# IAN WATSON (b. 1943) UK

## THE JONAH KIT (1975)

Overbearing Nobel Prize-winning physicist Paul Hammond is already regarded as an unwelcome genius when he makes his latest discovery. Grudgingly backed by his truculent colleagues and his unfaithful wife, Hammond invites the world's press to a radio observatory in Mexico where he announces that the universe is a phantom cosmos, a mere by-product of the true reality created by God. Earth therefore exists only by default and is even more contingent than mankind already suspected. As throngs of religious fanatics, the poor and outlaw bikers on chopped hogs gather outside the perimeter fence of the observatory, American agents visit Tokyo, where the Japanese authorities hold a boy who appears to have the consciousness of a lost astronaut melded with his own. Believing the child to be linked with a Soviet experiment to convert whales cybernetically into anti-submarine weapons, the scientists discover the truth about cetacean communication. The clicks of the cachalots not only resonate through the oceans of Earth but they echo events deep in the void of outer space.

As the above indicates, Ian Watson is a writer overflowing with notions and a veritable dam-burst of wayward concepts has gushed from his pen since the publication of his first book (*The Embedding*) in 1973. *The Jonah Kit* is typical of Watson's work – spiky, complex, adroitly written and both breathless and bracing in its willingness to scale intellectual heights. Equally at home in the social sciences as he was with the harder disciplines, Watson came to be regarded as the premier British SF writer of ideas in the seventies. Many younger authors owe him a considerable debt. Few genre novelists before him were willing to make such difficult demands on their readers or were able to provide such corresponding rewards. Today, intoxicating invention overload of the kind Watson pioneered is commonplace in SF writing. With its invigoratingly dyspeptic characters, *The Jonah Kit* is a striking reminder of the harshness of the mid-seventies, when the hippie dream had evanesced and our world began to face up to the problems that loom even larger now.

### ≋ Read on
*Miracle Visitors*
Ideas men: Paul Cornell, *British Summertime*; Robert Holdstock, *Where Time Winds Blow*; Rudy Rucker, *Spacetime Donuts*; John Varley, *The Ophiuci Hotline*

# H.G. WELLS (1866–1946) UK

## THE TIME MACHINE (1895)
Gathered around a dinner table in late 19th-century suburban London, a group of middle class and professional men listen to the theories about the nature of time expounded by one of their number. The theories sound fanciful until the man produces a miniature time machine and proceeds to make it vanish into thin air. A week later the guests, still sceptical, return and hear the fantastic story that their host, the Time Traveller, now has to relate. Using a larger version of his time machine, he has projected himself far into the future. In the world to

which the traveller journeys, man has evolved into two distinct species, the gentle and beautiful Eloi and the troglodytic Morlocks who emerge from their underground dwellings only when night falls. At first the lotus life led by the Eloi seems an idyllic one but the theft of his machine and his dawning awareness of the relationship between the Eloi and the Morlocks drive the Time Traveller to increasingly desperate attempts to return to his own time. After one final terrifying confrontation with the Morlocks, he recovers his machine and heads for home. Exhausted and bedraggled, he stumbles into the room in time to tell his tale. The next day, the Time Traveller vanishes again and no more is ever heard of him.

Like so much science fiction, the novella which made Wells's reputation is deeply rooted in the concerns of the period in which it was written. Late Victorian anxieties about the growing divide between the cultured classes and a supposed underclass in London's East End are clearly reflected in the relationship between the sybaritic Eloi and the darkly threatening Morlocks. Yet such is the power of Wells's imagination that *The Time Machine* transcends the particular circumstances that inspired it. More than a hundred years after its first publication, it remains one of the most compelling of all stories about voyages into the future.

📖 **Film versions:** *The Time Machine* (1960), *The Time Machine* (1978, TV movie), *The Time Machine* (2002)

📖 **Read on**

Chrononauts: ▶▶ William S. Burroughs, T*he Place of Dead Roads*; David Lake, *The Man Who Loved Morlocks*; Hilbert Schenck, *A Rose For Armageddon*; ▶▶ Bob Shaw, *The Two-Timers*; ▶▶ Roger Zelazny, *Roadmarks*

## THE ISLAND OF DR MOREAU (1896)

Solitary survivor of a shipwreck in the south Pacific, Edward Prendick is picked up by a boat heading for a remote island and is forced to accept the reluctantly offered hospitality of its overlord, a mysterious and sinister figure named Doctor Moreau. Moreau's only companions on the island are a disgraced and drunken former medical student, Montgomery, and a troop of misshapen men whose appearance both disgusts Prendick and arouses his curiosity. Who and what are they? Slowly the truth about the island dawns on him. Moreau has been conducting a series of vivisectionist experiments, striving to transform beast into man, and the deformed creatures are the results. Even more hideous beast-men lurk in the darker corners of Moreau's island. The devilish doctor has imposed a religion of a kind and a skin-deep morality on his creations, who struggle to emphasize their humanity, but the beast within is always ready to stir. When it does, even the god-like Moreau is in danger.

Like Wells's other 'scientific romances' of the 1890s, *The Island of Dr Moreau* seizes upon a topic that was at the forefront of scientific debate at the time and uses his extraordinarily vivid and wide-ranging imagination to give it new life in fictional form. In *The Time Machine* it was the nature of time and in *The War of the Worlds* it was the possibility of life on other planets. In *The Island of Dr Moreau* the topic was vivisection, then very much in the news headlines. By linking it with much older anxieties about man taking on the role of god (the sort that had fuelled ➤➤ Mary Shelley's *Frankenstein*), Wells created a narrative that continues to play on our fears about what, if anything, divides humanity from the animal world.

🎞 **Film versions:** *Island of Lost Souls* (1933), *The Island of Doctor Moreau* (1977), *The Island of Doctor Moreau* (1996)

📖 **Read on**

*The Invisible Man, The World Set Free, In the Days of the Comet*

## READONATHEME: ISLANDS

>> Brian Aldiss, *Moreau's Other Island*
>> J.G. Ballard, *Concrete Island*
   John Christopher, *A Wrinkle in the Skin*
   William Golding, *Lord of the Flies*
   Garry Kilworth, *The Roof of Voyaging*
>> Christopher Priest, *The Dream Archipelago*
   Lance Sieveking, *The Ultimate Island*
>> Kurt Vonnegut, *Galapagos*
>> Gene Wolfe, *The Island of Dr Death and Other Stories*
>> John Wyndham, *Web*

## THE WAR OF THE WORLDS (1898)

'Across the gulf of space, minds that are to our minds as ours are to those of the beasts that perish, intellects vast and cool and unsympathetic, regarded this earth with envious eyes, and slowly and surely drew their plans against us.' From the very first paragraph of his classic story of alien invasion, Wells establishes the awesome power of the Martians who are about to plunge England into chaos. Complacent assumptions of man's technological superiority are about to be shattered and Wells drags his readers into the midst of the confrontation between Earth and Mars at breakneck speed. The narrator of the story is one of those who witnesses the arrival of the invaders – their first ship lands on Horsell Common near Woking – and sees the catastrophe that ensues when a deputation attempts to approach them. Within seconds, the would-be peacemakers are incinerated by the Martian heat-rays. Within days, the repulsive, multi-tentacled Martians, hidden inside their gigantic, three-legged war machines, have marched across the home counties and the once-proud civilization of late Victorian England is in ruins. The narrator, stumbling into London after a succession of close escapes from the Martians, finds the imperial capital a near-deserted wasteland. Nothing it seems can stop the invaders...

In the best-known of his 'scientific romances', Wells takes an almost gleeful delight in depicting the swift destruction of contemporary civilization, as the Martians march relentlessly onwards, but he combines this with a gripping narrative of the central character's struggle for survival. Wells was the founding father of modern science fiction and his curiously ambivalent feelings about science and technology (in his novels they seem far less like the unambiguous forces for good they are in his writings on politics and society) have permeated the genre in the century since he was writing books like *The War of the Worlds*. In this, as in so many other ways, Wells the pioneer created the template which other writers have copied.

◀ **Film versions:** *The War of the Worlds* (1953), *War of the Worlds* (2005)

## ⚵ Read on

*The First Men in the Moon*

Invaders: ➤➤ Brian Aldiss, *The Interpreter*; Garry Kilworth, *In Solitary*; ➤➤ Larry Niven and Jerry Pournelle, *Footfall*; Eric Frank Russell, *Three to Conquer*; ➤➤ Theodore Sturgeon, *The Cosmic Rape*

# KATE WILHELM (b. 1928) USA

## WHERE LATE THE SWEET BIRDS SANG (1976)

In a remote rural area of upstate Washington the comfortable Sumner farming clan found a research hospital with government backing. While the world slips into economic collapse, worsened by widespread pollution and escalating military action, David Sumner completes his studies in genetics at Harvard University and returns home to work in the hospital. As a lethal epidemic spreads across America, leaving the survivors sterile, David works against time to perfect the ultimate survival strategy for an increasingly barren, gradually declining human race: cloning. As limited nuclear war begins and the isolated community sees its numbers dwindle, David's research bears fruit – grown in tanks under computer control, cloned embryos reach post-uterine age. The immediate survival of the colony is guaranteed, but experiments with mice show that the fourth generation of clones would not be viable. Contact with the outside world ceases as civilization falls silent. As the clones mature, gradually taking over the settlement, David and his contemporaries realize that these inheritors of the Earth are different:

like identical twins, they share more than just the same genes. With each new generation the Clones become more like facets of a single organism than individuals, sharing emotions and attitudes. But a child is born into the community who will either be the salvation of the Clones by helping them raid the dead cities for scientific materials or prove their undoing, as he is a singular being whose individuality is as perilous to himself as it is to his hosts.

Kate Wilhelm is currently recognized for her confident crime novels that are bestsellers in the USA, while until the early eighties she was best known as one of the leading female writers of SF; she was married to Damon Knight, the noted SF author, critic and anthologist. *Where Late the Sweet Birds Sang* is generally regarded as the finest treatment of cloning in literature to date, its becalmed tone and lambent three-act structure providing an unhysterical reminder that to be human is to be unique and that to be different is sublime.

## 🕮 Read on
*The Killing Thing, Let the Fire Fall*
Clones: C.J. Cherryh, *Cyteen*; Richard Cowper, *Clone*; Kazuo Ishiguro, *Never Let Me Go*

# JACK WILLIAMSON (b. 1908) USA

## THE LEGION OF TIME (1938)

1927: Denny Lanning is suddenly confronted by a vision of a beautiful girl in white holding a stupendous crystal, in which she reveals a utopian city of the future. After she warns our hero that a woman of malevolent aspect will shortly appear to tempt him, he indeed experiences another manifestation when an equally bewitching yet martial maiden in red armour materializes before his astonished eyes. Both women represent different possible fates for Earth and Lanning is the fulcrum upon which reality itself will pivot. Each scenario exists only as a probability and Lanning's actions will determine if the civilization of the lady in white or the dystopia of the scarlet siren will prevail. Ten years later, while flying a plane over China in the war against Japan, Lanning is about to perish when an uncanny ship coalesces out of nowhen: *The Chronion* is crewed by a legion of dead men, travelling into the alternate futures of Earth along the geodesic arcs of probability. Lanning is about to commit himself to the final, terrible battle that will decide which world shall triumph and which woman will be his.

Although it is far from being one of Williamson's best written works, *The Legion of Time* has a raw vitality and entertainment value typical of its time. Most significantly, it extrapolates a theory that was later conceived by a physicist in the fifties: Hugh Everett proposed a parallel worlds hypothesis to account for some of the vagaries of quantum mechanics, similar to that described in Williamson's book. Science writer John Gribbin has praised Williamson's early understanding of quantum theory and the latter's command of the ideas is impressive. Although social SF often yields prescient metaphors for changes sparked by the evolution of technology, cases of hard SF actually anticipating fundamental theories concerning the nature of reality itself are rare, hence our belief that *The Legion of Time* is a seminal book. Williamson has continued to write in the genre regularly until the present, the last survivor of the Golden Age of magazine SF, providing a sense of continuity to the field since the 1920s.

### ⮒ Read on

Time travel variations: ›› Barrington J. Bayley, *Collision With Chronos*, *The Fall of Chronopolis*; ›› Michael Bishop, *No Enemy But Time*; David Gerrold, *The Man Who Folded Himself*; ›› Connie Willis, *Lincoln's Dreams*

# CONNIE WILLIS (b. 1945) USA

## DOOMSDAY BOOK (1992)

In mid 21st-century Oxford historians have an extra research tool which they can use. Time travel has become possible and academics are able to journey back into the past to observe the period they are studying at first hand. Some ages are deemed more dangerous than others for travellers and the 14th century, with its record of plague and pestilence, has a particularly low rating as a destination. Despite this, and despite the misgivings of Dunworthy, one of her tutors, research student Kivrin Engle travels back, supposedly to the date 1320. Something goes radically wrong. On arriving Kivrin is taken ill and confined to a small village near Oxford with a nobleman's family that has retreated to the country to escape a mysterious epidemic. Meanwhile, back in the 21st century, there are more problems. The technician who arranged Kivrin's journey has succumbed to an unidentified virus, Oxford itself has been placed under quarantine and Dunworthy and his colleagues are facing a race against time to rescue Kivrin from the past.

Connie Willis is one of the most successful writers of speculative fiction of the past thirty years, winner of several Hugo and Nebula awards, and this ingeniously constructed amalgam of science fiction and historical fiction shows her at her best. The narrative moves seamlessly between the future and the past, creating a growing tension in both the world Kivrin has left and the one in which she has arrived. In many of her novels, Connie Willis writes with an amiable, offbeat sense of humour and this is occasionally in evidence in *Doomsday Book*, but the story of love and loss and the inexplicable mysteries of human suffering has a power and a poignancy that is unmatched in her other works. Particularly in its last hundred pages, *Doomsday Book* is as moving and engrossing a narrative as any in contemporary American fiction.

### 🕮 Read on

*To Say Nothing of the Dog, Fire Watch*
L. Sprague De Camp, *Lest Darkness Fall*; Robert Holdstock, *Earthwind*; Jack London, *The Star Rover*; ›› Keith Roberts, *The Chalk Giants*; Mark Twain, *A Connecticut Yankee in King Arthur's Court*

# GENE WOLFE (b. 1931) USA

## THE SHADOW OF THE TORTURER (1980)

The setting is Urth, our planet in the very distant future, a place so old that many of the original meanings of artefacts and customs have been forgotten. Consequently, Urth is a world bound by elaborate ritual and inexplicable tradition, apparently governed by mysticism that is merely archaic science. Within the walled citadel of Nessus, one of the rococo towers which are the remains of ancient rockets provides a home for the young Severian, who endures an education as a neophyte in the Torturers' Guild. Studying the dark discipline of his craft, the ambivalent Severian grows toward an adulthood fraught with peril while promising glory. His eventual betrayal of his duty will take this indolent anti-hero on a quest across his strangely medieval technoplane, see him immersed in the hell of war before ascending to the coveted position of Autarch. Yet Severian has always realized his true significance in the shape of things: even this lofty authority will be surpassed as he reaches his apotheosis, a moment of revelation that will alter Urth forever.

*The Shadow of the Torturer* is the first volume of *The Book of the New Sun* series. Initially published in four parts, the story is now available as two omnibuses. This massive novel has been hailed as one of the most important efforts of imaginative literature ever. In scope, symbolism and popularity it has been favourably compared to *The Lord of the Rings*, Mervyn Peake's monumental and unfinished *Gormenghast* trilogy and *Dune*. As these parallels suggest, *The Book of the New Sun* has quasi-historical and spiritual overtones that have meant some critics have considered it sword and sorcery fantasy. More properly the book is maybe the greatest representative yet of the 'Dying Earth' group of science fantasies, an ambiguous borderland of imaginative literature where science and magic are combined or misinterpreted. Gene Wolfe is undoubtedly one of the most elegant and ambitious authors in the annals of speculative fiction. Readers of baroque fantasy prose stylists will relish his award-winning titles that are equally worthy successor of both Borges and C.S. Lewis.

### ⮑ Read on

The rest of *The Book of the New Sun*: *The Claw of the Conciliator*, *The Sword of the Lictor* and *The Citadel of the Autarch*

'Dying Earth' science fantasy collections: ➤➤ M. John Harrison, *Viriconium*; ➤➤ Jack Vance, *Tales of the Dying Earth*; ➤➤ Michael Moorcock, *The Dancers at the End of Time*; Clark Ashton Smith, *The Emperor of Dreams*

# JOHN WYNDHAM (1903–69) UK

## THE MIDWICH CUCKOOS (1957)

Returning from a trip to London, author Richard Gayford and his wife find the road to Midwich barred by the authorities. No one who has entered the village for twenty-four hours has returned. Determined to get home, the Gayfords sneak across a field. The next thing the couple know, they are hauled, unconscious, back across an invisible barrier – a huge bubble of odourless gas appears to have settled over Midwich. Suddenly dissipating, the gas seems to leave the rural community relatively unharmed, until it becomes clear several months later that every woman of childbearing age in Midwich is pregnant. Gayford and local philosopher Zellaby observe the phenomenon in a semi-official capacity. Soon the babies are born, perfect apart from their golden eyes. Gradually it becomes clear to the residents of Midwich that the cuckoo-children are a unique brood indeed, capable of imposing their will upon their host parents. As their power grows with age, the village ineffectually debates the morality of what should be done about these strangers.

John Wyndham had already electrified Britain and America with three compelling bestsellers when he produced his finest novel. Prior to this he had written numerous novels and short stories for the US pulps before modifying his approach to that of the traditional English novel: *The Day of the Triffids*, *The Kraken Wakes* and *The Chrysalids* found Wyndham a wide audience outside the magazines among general readers who found his familiar settings, genteel prose and sheer Englishness to be all they needed to enjoy science fiction. By making the genre palatable again, Wyndham helped remind the mainstream of the long history of SF before the pulps, connecting them with the tradition of Wells, Huxley and Orwell. Throughout the sixties, when his critical reputation (if not his popularity) waned, Wyndham became regarded as a somewhat conservative purveyor of 'cosy catastrophes', inward-looking Empire-in-decline metaphors. But Wyndham held a massive influence over English New Wave writers and it is now recognized that he was in fact a Darwinist with some expedient ideas of how to deal with intra-species conflicts, as the unsentimental climaxes of *The Chrysalids* and *The Midwich Cuckoos* make plain. His eminently readable and entertaining work remains relevant today as the West struggles with complex issues of post-imperialism, multiculturalism and terrorism.

**⬛ Film versions:** *Village of the Damned* (1960), *Village of the Damned* (1995)

**⬛ Read on**
*The Day of the Triffids*, *Consider Her Ways*, *Exiles on Asperus* (collection of novellas which includes two of his pre-war stories)
SF by mainstream writers: Peter Ackroyd, *First Light*; Michael Frayn, *A Very Private Life*; Doris Lessing, *Shikasta*; David Mitchell, *Cloud Atlas*; Audrey Niffenegger, *The Time Traveller's Wife*

# ROGER ZELAZNY (1937–95) USA

## THIS IMMORTAL (aka …AND CALL ME CONRAD) (1966)

Centuries after the three-day war, a ruined Earth is largely uninhabited, reduced to a tourist spot for the Vegans, humanoid aliens quietly oppressing mankind simply by being its cultural superiors. While many *Homo Sapiens* elect to live offplanet, residing on Saturn's moon Titan or more distant worlds, content to accept the intellectual hegemony of Vega, Conrad Nomikos is one of the minority remaining at home. Tall, club-footed, his visage blighted by a fungal growth contracted at a radioactive hot spot, Nomikos works as Arts Commissioner for Earth, rediscovering and curating the remnants of its once glorious history. Wryly spoken and ironically mannered, Nomikos is hiding something a few are beginning to openly suspect: as lethal in combat as he is erudite, this Greek aesthete is a mutant several hundred years old. When Nomikos is chosen to accompany Myshtigo, the Vegan's greatest living writer on tour around the Mediterranean, it seems that more than a guidebook for the aliens will be the result. Nomikos believes Myshtigo will pen a survey of Earth reinforcing its parochial status as a traveller's curiosity, silencing the few dissenting Terrans who dream of restoring their homeworld to its former importance. But Nomikos understands that merely assassinating Myshtigo will not serve the cause he has covertly supported for centuries – if humanity is to regain its birthright, subtler means will be required.

Zelazny's first novel is the ideal place to begin exploring this singular writer. Displaying an informed, witty understanding of mythological archetypes, *This Immortal* utilizes its Hellenistic setting and Classical avatars to splendid advantage. Elegant and flavoursome, this book is representative of the author's oblique attack, possessing a concise, edgy quality often absent in works employing styles as ornate as Zelazny's. This astringency contrasts wonderfully with his more poetic moments, becoming more pronounced in his 1970s' work. Rising to prominence as a blinding light of America's New Wave alongside ❱❱ Delany and ❱❱ Ellison, Zelazny was highly regarded within the field, even collaborating with elder statesmen like ❱❱ Bester and ❱❱ Dick. Although his 1960s' work is his most fêted, his untimely death in 1995 robbed imaginative writing of one of its most fascinating eminences.

## ❧ Read on

Classic Zelazny: *Lord of Light*, *The Dream Master*, *Today We Choose Faces*

Oblique American New Wavers: ❱❱ Samuel R. Delany, *The Einstein Intersection*; James Sallis, *Time's Hammers*

# READONATHEME COUNTLESS TOMORROWS

Immortality and life after life

- ›› Alfred Bester, *Extro* (aka *The Computer Connection*)
- ›› Philip José Farmer, *Traitor to the Living*
  James Gunn, *The Immortals*
  George Bernard Shaw, *Back To Methuselah*
- ›› Lucius Shepard, *Green Eyes*
- ›› Robert Silverberg, *Recalled to Life*
  Michael Marshall Smith, *Spares*
- ›› Jack Vance, *To Live Forever*
- ›› A.E. Van Vogt, *The Weapon Shops of Isher*
  Robert Anton Wilson and Robert Shea, *The Illuminatus Trilogy*
- ›› Gene Wolfe, *Peace*
- ›› John Wyndham, *Trouble With Lichen*

# SCIENCEFICTIONAWARDS

## THE HUGO AWARD FOR BEST SF NOVEL

The World Science Fiction Achievement Awards (nicknamed in honour of Hugo Gernsback) have been presented annually since 1953 at the World Science Fiction Convention and are decided by votes cast by readers joining the World Science Fiction Association. The main award is for Best Novel, but there are other prizes for shorter fiction and SF works in non-literary media. The most coveted of the many SF awards presented worldwide, Hugos are rarely awarded to New Wave authors and many important writers who have won numerous prizes (such as ›› Silverberg and ›› Ellison) have only won the Hugo for short fiction. As the Worldcon usually takes place in America, US authors tend to have the advantage in winning Hugos. Occasionally, fantasy works win Hugos.

Note: There were no Hugo Awards in 1954 or 1957.

1953   ››Alfred Bester, *The Demolished Ma*n
1955     Mark Clifton and Frank Riley, *They'd Rather Be Right*
1956   ››Robert A. Heinlein, *Double Star*
1958     Fritz Leiber, *The Big Time*
1959   ››James Blish, *A Case of Conscience*
1960   ››Robert A. Heinlein, *Starship Troopers*
1961   ››Walter M. Miller Jr, *A Canticle For Leibowitz*
1962   ››Robert A. Heinlein, *Stranger in a Strange Land*

1963   &raquo;Philip K. Dick, *The Man in the High Castle*

1964    Clifford D. Simak, *Way Station*

1965    Fritz Leiber, *The Wanderer*

1966   &raquo;Roger Zelazny, *This Immortal*/&raquo; Frank Herbert, *Dune* (tie)

1967   &raquo;Robert A. Heinlein, *The Moon is a Harsh Mistress*

1968   &raquo;Roger Zelazny, *Lord of Light*

1969   &raquo;John Brunner, *Stand on Zanzibar*

1970   &raquo;Ursula K. Le Guin, *The Left Hand of Darkness*

1971   &raquo;Larry Niven, *Ringworld*

1972   &raquo;Philip José Farmer, *To Your Scattered Bodies Go*

1973   &raquo;Isaac Asimov, *The Gods Themselves*

1974   &raquo;Arthur C. Clarke, *Rendezvous With Rama*

1975   &raquo;Ursula K. Le Guin, *The Dispossessed*

1976   &raquo;Joe Haldeman, *The Forever War*

1977   &raquo;Kate Wilhelm, *Where Late the Sweet Birds Sang*

1978   &raquo;Frederik Pohl, *Gateway*

1979    Vonda N. MacIntyre, *Dreamsnake*

1980   &raquo;Arthur C. Clarke, *The Fountains of Paradise*

1981    Joan D. Vinge, *The Snow Queen*

1982    C.J. Cherryh, *Downbelow Station*

1983   &raquo;Isaac Asimov, *Foundation's Edge*

1984    David Brin, *Startide Rising*

1985   &raquo;William Gibson, *Neuromancer*

1986   &raquo;Orson Scott Card, *Ender's Game*

1987   &raquo;Orson Scott Card, *Speaker For the Dead*

1988    David Brin, *The Uplift War*

1989    C.J. Cherryh, *Cyteen*

| | |
|---|---|
| 1990 | Dan Simmons, *Hyperion* |
| 1991 | Lois McMaster Bujold, *The Vor Game* |
| 1992 | Lois McMaster Bujold, *Barrayar* |
| 1993 | ≫Vernor Vinge, *A Fire Upon the Deep*/≫ Connie Willis, *The Doomsday Book* (tie) |
| 1994 | ≫Kim Stanley Robinson, *Green Mars* |
| 1995 | Lois McMaster Bujold, *Mirror Dance* |
| 1996 | ≫Neal Stephenson, *The Diamond Age* |
| 1997 | ≫Kim Stanley Robinson, *Blue Mars* |
| 1998 | ≫Joe Haldeman, *Forever Peace* |
| 1999 | ≫Connie Willis, *To Say Nothing of the Dog* |
| 2000 | ≫Vernor Vinge, *A Deepness in the Sky* |
| 2001 | J.K. Rowling, *Harry Potter and the Goblet of Fire* |
| 2002 | Neil Gaiman, *American Gods* |
| 2003 | Robert J. Sawyer, *Hominids* |
| 2004 | Lois McMaster Bujold, *Paladin of Souls* |
| 2005 | Susanna Clarke, *Jonathan Strange & Mr Norrell* |

## NEBULA AWARD FOR BEST SF NOVEL

Nebula Awards have been presented annually since 1965 and are voted upon by The Science Fiction Writers of America, a body of professional authors and editors. The main award is for Best Novel, but there are categories for shorter forms. Fantasy works sometimes win the Nebulas. The closest UK equivalent is the ›› Arthur C. Clarke Award, given since 1987.

Note: Qualifying and prizegiving dates for Nebulas differ from those for Hugos, so the same book can win both awards a year apart.

1965 ››Frank Herbert, *Dune*

1966 ››Daniel Keyes, *Flowers For Algernon*/›› Samuel R. Delany, *Babel 17* (tie)

1967 ››Samuel R. Delany, *The Einstein Intersection* (aka *A Fabulous, Formless Darkness*)

1968    Alexei Panshin, *Rite of Passage*

1969 ››Ursula K. Le Guin, *The Left Hand of Darkness*

1970 ››Larry Niven, *Ringworld*

1971 ››Robert Silverberg, *A Time of Changes*

1972 ››Isaac Asimov, *The Gods Themselves*

1973 ››Arthur C. Clarke, *Rendezvous With Rama*

1974 ››Ursula K. Le Guin, *The Dispossessed*

1975 ››Joe Haldeman, *The Forever War*

1976 ››Frederik Pohl, *Man Plus*

1977 ››Frederik Pohl, *Gateway*

1978    Vonda N. McIntyre, *Dreamsnake*

1979 ››Arthur C. Clarke, *The Fountains of Paradise*

1980 ››Gregory Benford, *Timescape*

1981 ››Gene Wolfe, *The Claw of the Conciliator*

1982 ≫Michael Bishop, *No Enemy But Time*

1983 David Brin, *Startide Rising*

1984 ≫William Gibson, *Neuromancer*

1985 ≫Orson Scott Card, *Ender's Game*

1986 ≫Orson Scott Card, *Speaker For the Dead*

1987 Pat Murphy, *The Falling Woman*

1988 Lois McMaster Bujold, *Falling Free*

1989 Elizabeth Ann Scarborough, *The Healer's War*

1990 ≫Ursula K. Le Guin, *Tehanu*

1991 ≫Michael Swanwick, *Stations of the Tide*

1992 ≫Connie Willis, *The Doomsday Book*

1993 ≫Kim Stanley Robinson, *Red Mars*

1994 ≫Greg Bear, *Moving Mars*

1995 Robert J. Sawyer, *The Terminal Experiment* (aka *Hobson's Choice*)

1996 Nicola Griffith, *Slow River*

1997 Vonda N. McIntyre, *The Moon and the Sun*

1998 ≫Joe Haldeman, *Forever Peace*

1999 Octavia Butler, *Parable of the Talents*

2000 ≫Greg Bear, *Darwin's Radio*

2001 Catherine Asaro, *The Quantum Rose*

2002 Neil Gaiman, *American Gods*

2003 Elizabeth Moon, *Speed of Dark*

2004 Lois McMaster Bujold, *Paladin of Souls*

2005 Joe Haldeman, *Camouflage*

## BRITISH SCIENCE FICTION ASSOCIATION (BSFA) AWARDS FOR BEST NOVEL

The UK equivalent of the Hugos, voted for by British fans.

Note: There were no BSFA awards for best novel in 1971 or 1972.

1969  ≫John Brunner, *Stand on Zanzibar*

1970  ≫John Brunner, *The Jagged Orbit*

1973  ≫Arthur C. Clarke, *Rendezvous With Rama*

1974  ≫Christopher Priest, *Inverted World*

1975  ≫Bob Shaw, *Orbitsville*

1976    Michael Coney, *Brontomek*

1977  ≫Ian Watson, *The Jonah Kit*

1978  ≫Philip K. Dick, *A Scanner Darkly*

1979  ≫J.G. Ballard, *The Unlimited Dream Company*

1980  ≫Gregory Benford, *Timescape*

1981  ≫Gene Wolfe, *The Shadow of the Torturer*

1982  ≫Brian Aldiss, *Helliconia Spring*

1983  ≫John Sladek, *Tik-Tok*

1984    Robert Holdstock, *Mythago Wood*

1985  ≫Brian Aldiss, *Helliconia Winter*

1986  ≫Bob Shaw, *The Ragged Astronauts*

1987  ≫Keith Roberts, *Grainne*

1988    Robert Holdstock, *Lavondyss*

1989    Terry Pratchett, *Pyramids*

1990    Colin Greenland, *Take Back Plenty*

1991    Dan Simmons, *The Fall of Hyperion*

1992  ≫Kim Stanley Robinson, *Red Mars*

1993    Christopher Evans, *Aztec Century*

1994 ›› Iain M. Banks, *Feersum Enjinn*
1995 ›› Stephen Baxter, *The Time Ships*
1996 ›› Iain M. Banks, *Excession*
1997   Mary Doria Russell, *The Sparrow*
1998 ›› Christopher Priest, *The Extremes*
1999   Ken MacLeod, *The Sky Road*
2000   Mary Gentle, *Ash: A Secret History*
2001   Alastair Reynolds, *Chasm City*
2002 ›› Christopher Priest, *The Separation*
2003   Jon Courtnay Grimwood, *Fellaheen*
2004   Ian MacDonald, *River of Gods*
2005   Geoff Ryman, *Air*

# ABRIEFGLOSSARYOF SFTERMS

\* indicates a separate entry.

**AI** Artificial intelligence, indicating a computer or robot\* capable of independent (even creative) thought that goes beyond that dictated by its basic programming.

**Alternative history** SF that relies upon the outcome of a pivotal event in history being different from that of its real-world equivalent to create its setting, such as the Axis powers winning instead of losing the Second World War. Less pure variants use time travel and/or the parallel worlds theories of quantum physics to explore alternative histories.

**Android** Originally interchangeable with 'robot'\*, android is now used primarily to indicate a biological artificial human AI\* created through manufacturing processes and/or genetic engineering.

**Campbellian SF** see the entry on ❯❯ John W. Campbell. *See also* Genre SF, Hard SF.

**Clone** A laboratory-spawned being created from the genetic material of another individual, in SF usually physically identical to its original genetic donor.

**Cyborg** A cybernetic organism, a combination of both machine and flesh.

**Cyberpunk** The movement in 1980s' genre SF that combined the attitude of punk rock musicians, the literary quality of New Wave writing, the influence of American hardboiled crime fiction and the technological content of hard* SF.

**Cyberspace** The virtual reality* matrix of the internet – the non-existent space where computers interface with each other. In SF cyberspace is often explored directly by the consciousness of characters using advanced information technology.

**Dystopia** A society that is nightmarish or inhuman in character as a result of political oppression and/or unchecked technological overload and ecological collapse. The opposite of a utopia.*

**Extrasolar** Something that originates from outside Earth's solar system.

**Fantasy** The genre of imaginative writing that uses the magic of the supernatural to distinguish itself from realistic mainstream fiction – unlike SF, which utilizes the natural qualities of rationality and science to separate itself from the mainstream.

**Genre** A particular category of fiction that is distinguishable from mainstream literature by its primary focus on a particular area, e.g. westerns, crime fiction, SF.

**Genre SF** Science fiction that was published in or has arisen from the models established in the American pulp magazines* that flourished from 1925 to 1965 and writing published in books labelled and marketed as science fiction.

**Gestalt entity** Also known as a 'hive mind', used in SF to indicate the group consciousness of telepathic mutants or the collective intelligence of aliens whose mental status as individuals is debatable.

**Golden Age** See the entry on ›› John W. Campbell. *See also* Genre SF, Hard SF.

**Hard SF** Traditional genre SF that focuses on the technological sciences such as physics, engineering, biology and mathematics, as opposed to **Soft SF**, which concentrates on the human sciences of sociology, psychology and politics.

**Literary SF** As opposed to genre SF, literary SF is science fiction published outside the pulp magazines and in books not labelled as SF, sometimes by authors not usually associated with the genre. Also, SF writing of higher literary quality than routine genre SF that may nevertheless have been written by authors who started publishing in genre SF magazines/SF book imprints.

**Mainstream** The main body of general fiction written and published outside genre conventions and genre markets, commonly regarded as more serious and accomplished by the majority of literary critics and general readers with little firsthand experience of genre fiction.

**Mutant** An individual born with differing physical abilities and/or characteristics than the majority of its species due to an evolutionary genetic quirk or an unusual influence on its parents' environment.

**New Wave** The literary SF of the mid-sixties onwards that insisted upon the need for writing that was comparable to the best of mainstream fiction, using experimental techniques imported from Modernist texts. The New Wave also focused on contemporary subjects considered too politically contentious or downbeat by the majority of traditional ❯❯ Campbellian genre SF writers.

**Planetary romance** Colourful, romantic stories of adventure on alien worlds, sometimes employing fantasy symbols such as swords, originating from the early pulp magazines.*

**Post-holocaust SF** Stories set in the aftermath of the widespread nuclear war that would destroy our civilization.

**Proto SF** Works of literature that some critics claim for the genre, written before the acceptance of the scientific method by society at large or before the widespread use of the term 'science fiction'.

**Psi, psionic** Interchangeable blanket terms for the theoretical mental powers of extra-sensory perception (ESP) that some SF writers have suggested might be the next phase of human evolution. **Telepathy** is the reading of (or nonverbal communication between) human minds, **telekinesis** is the ability to move objects with the mind alone, **telempathy** is the ability to experience the emotions of others, while 'precogs' have the ability to foretell possible future events.

**Pulp magazines** The popular mass-market American magazines that appeared at the end of the 19th century. The pulps showcased and separated popular fiction into the different genres we recognize today.

**Robot** A word coined for the 1923 SF play *R.U.R.* by Czech writers Josef and Karel Capek to describe a human-shaped machine, sometimes an AI,* created by mechanical and electronic engineering with no biological components.

**Science fantasy** Genre works where science and magic are both used by the writer, prevalent in far future settings such as ❯❯ Jack Vance's *The Dying Earth* or sword and sorcery-tinged titles like ❯❯ Michael Moorcock's *Hawkmoon*.

**Soft SF** *see* Hard SF.

**Space opera** Epic, sometimes baroque sagas of majestic sweep of space travel, galactic empires, heroes and villains that originated in the early days of the pulp magazines.* Space opera is what the general public immediately identifies as being the essence and limits of SF, since much early magazine SF, *Star Wars* and *Star Trek* all provide classic examples of this form.

**Sword and sorcery** Also known as 'heroic fantasy', the most prevalent form of fantasy writing that focuses on heroism, quests and symbols such as swords, dragons, wizards and little people as typified by the works of Robert E. Howard and J.R.R. Tolkien.

**Telepathy, telekinesis** etc *see* Psi, psionic.

**Terra** Latin for 'Earth', this word was widely used by characters created by genre SF writers in the 1930s and 1940s.

**Utopia** An ideal society of peace and prosperity for all, probably achieved through brilliant social engineering. The literal meaning of the word utopia is 'nowhere'. *See also* Dystopia.

**VR** or **virtual reality** A computer-generated dreamspace used to simulate reality for a user who interfaces their consciousness with the appropriate technology. Flight simulators and computer games are example models for VR in SF.

# INDEX